Contents

The publishers would like to thank the following authors for their
retellings of the full-length Classic stories:
Joan Cameron (The Three Musketeers); Marie Stuart (Gulliver's Travels);
Joyce Faraday (Treasure Island); Brenda Ralph Lewis and Ronne Randall (Oliver Twist);
John Grant (Robin Hood).

The woodcuts were individually hand carved in box wood by Jonathan Mercer
(The Three Musketeers, Treasure Island, Oliver Twist).

Line illustrations by John Lawrence (Gulliver's Travels, Robin Hood).

Material used in this book was previously published as part of the
Ladybird Classics and Classic Fables and Legends series.

A catalogue record for this book is available from the British Library

Published by Ladybird Books Ltd Loughborough Leicestershire UK
Ladybird Books Ltd is a subsidiary of the Penguin Group of companies
© LADYBIRD BOOKS LTD MCMXCVI
LADYBIRD and the device of a Ladybird are trademarks of Ladybird Books Ltd

Classic Adventure Stories

Ladybird

THE THREE MUSKETEERS

by Alexandre Dumas
illustrated by David Barnett

D'ARTAGNAN

One morning in April, 1625, the little French town of Meung was in a state of great excitement. In those times, fighting was common in France. The King fought Richelieu, an ambitious cardinal. Noble families fought among themselves, and Spain was always ready to wage war with France. Few days passed without trouble in some town or another.

On this day, a crowd had gathered outside the town's inn. The cause of all the stir was the arrival of a young man on a very odd horse. It looked so comical that many of the townspeople wanted to laugh. Only the length of the sword at the young man's side, and the proud gleam in his eye, stopped them.

The young man was called D'Artagnan. He was on his way to Paris, where he hoped to fulfil his dearest wish – to become a King's Musketeer. His father had given him a letter to Monsieur de Tréville, an old friend who was now Captain of the Musketeers.

As he dismounted, D'Artagnan caught sight of a gentleman with a scar on his temple sitting at a window of the inn, talking to two other men. They were laughing, and D'Artagnan was sure that

A crowd had gathered

they were laughing at him. This was more than the impetuous young man could bear.

'Are you laughing at me?' challenged D'Artagnan, drawing his sword.

'I laugh as I please,' the man replied, turning away from the window and reappearing in the doorway.

D'Artagnan lunged at him in anger. Startled, the other man drew his sword. At the same moment, the innkeeper and several onlookers, anxious to prevent a fight, fell upon D'Artagnan. He was knocked senseless in the struggle and was carried indoors for attention.

When the innkeeper returned, the gentleman with the scar asked how, and who, the young man was.

'He will soon recover,' replied the innkeeper. 'I don't know who he is, sir, but he carries a letter to Monsieur de Tréville in Paris.'

'Indeed!' the other man said. 'I would like to see that letter. Where is it now?'

'In the young man's doublet, which is in the kitchen,' replied the innkeeper. 'The young man himself,' he added slyly, 'is upstairs, having his wounds seen to by my wife.'

'Prepare my bill and saddle

my horse,' said the gentleman as he rushed off to the kitchen. 'I am meeting Milady shortly, and then I must leave.'

Soon afterwards D'Artagnan limped into the courtyard. The first thing he saw was the gentleman, talking to a beautiful young woman in a carriage.

'What are the Cardinal's orders?' the young woman was asking.

'You must return to England at once,' the gentleman replied. 'Keep a close watch on the Duke of Buckingham, and inform the Cardinal as soon as he leaves London. I am returning to Paris.'

D'Artagnan rushed forward. 'Stand and fight, sir!' he demanded. 'Would you dare run away from me in front of a woman?'

Seeing her companion reach for his sword, Milady touched his arm. 'Remember,' she said quietly, 'delay could ruin our plans.'

'You are right,' he agreed. 'Go on your way, and I will go on mine.'

With that, the carriage moved off, the driver cracking his whip. The gentleman jumped on his horse and galloped away in the opposite direction.

'Coward!' D'Artagnan called after him, but the gentleman had gone.

D'Artagnan was ready to leave for Paris when he discovered that his letter to Monsieur de Tréville was missing.

'My letter!' he exclaimed. 'It's gone!'

The innkeeper quickly proclaimed his innocence. 'That gentleman must have taken it, sir,' he said. 'He showed great interest in it.'

Whoever had taken it, the letter seemed to be gone for good. All D'Artagnan could do was hope that Monsieur de Tréville would see him without it.

AT MONSIEUR DE TRÉVILLE'S

Monsieur de Tréville was a close friend of King Louis XIII. In those troubled times, the ruler of France needed this brave man at his side. De Tréville led the King's Musketeers, a band of bold men dedicated to protecting their King.

De Tréville's greatest rival for the King's favour was the cunning Cardinal Richelieu, a man nearly as powerful as the King himself. The Cardinal had his own company of Guards, who were bitter enemies of the Musketeers. The two companies' battles often ended in death.

Monsieur de Tréville's headquarters was always full of Musketeers. When D'Artagnan arrived, he made his way through them, his heart beating with excitement. D'Artagnan had to wait to see Monsieur de Tréville. He was scolding three of his men.

'Athos! Porthos! Aramis! I hear you were fighting in the streets and were arrested by the Cardinal's Guards. This will not do!'

'But they attacked us!' the three protested. 'We fought back, and escaped.'

'The Cardinal didn't tell me that,' murmured Monsieur de Tréville. 'But I will not let my men risk their lives for nothing. Brave men are dear to the King, and his Musketeers are the bravest of them all. Now go, and I will see this young man.'

Eagerly, D'Artagnan introduced himself and told Monsieur de Tréville about the stolen letter. He explained that he had come to Paris to join the Musketeers.

'I am afraid that won't be possible until you've proven your worth,' said Monsieur de Tréville. 'No one becomes a Musketeer without first serving in a lesser regiment. But because I liked your father,' he went on, 'I will do my best to help you. First, you will go to the Royal Academy to learn horsemanship and the art of the sword. Then we will see how you get on.'

'You won't be disappointed, I promise you, sir,' said D'Artagnan, bowing.

As he rushed from the Captain's headquarters, D'Artagnan encountered, one after the other, the three Musketeers who had been censored by Monsieur de Tréville. Still smarting from the scolding they had received, they took offence easily, and D'Artagnan, excited and impatient, managed to upset each of them in turn. He found himself challenged to three duels that very afternoon – the first with Athos at noon, another with Porthos at one o'clock and the third with Aramis at two o'clock.

Dismayed, D'Artagnan said to himself, 'I can't draw back. But if I am killed, at least I shall be killed by a Musketeer!'

A SURPRISE ENCOUNTER

D'Artagnan knew no one in Paris. He went to meet Athos alone, determined to fight well. But when Athos arrived, he brought the other two Musketeers with him. All three were astonished to see that they were to fight the same man.

'Now that you are here, gentlemen,' D'Artagnan said, 'I wish to apologise.'

At the word 'apologise' he saw contempt appear in their faces. They thought him a coward. His hot blood rose.

'You don't understand,' he protested. 'I apologise only in case I cannot fight all three of you! Monsieur Athos has the right to kill me first. And now – *en garde*!' With the most gallant air possible, D'Artagnan drew his sword. Athos had just drawn his when a company of the Cardinal's Guards appeared.

'Sheathe your swords!' called Porthos and Aramis together, but it was too late.

'Fighting, Musketeers?' cried one of the guards mockingly. 'You know that duelling is against the law. Put up your swords. I arrest you in the name of the King.'

'Never!' called the three Musketeers. 'There may be only three of us, but we will fight!'

'You are wrong – there are four of us,' said D'Artagnan quietly. 'Try me.'

'And what's your name, brave fellow?' asked Athos.

'D'Artagnan, monsieur.'

'Well then, Athos, Porthos, Aramis and D'Artagnan – forward!'

Swords clashed as the men fought fiercely, but at last the guards were beaten off and the four returned to Monsieur de Tréville's headquarters. 'I am not yet a Musketeer,' D'Artagnan thought, 'but at least I might be an apprentice.'

The incident caused a great fuss. Monsieur de Tréville scolded his

Musketeers in public, but congratulated them in private. The King heard of it and was so impressed by D'Artagnan's bravery that he placed him as a cadet in the Guards of Monsieur d'Essart.

From then on D'Artagnan and the three Musketeers were the greatest of friends. He learned about life in Paris, and about the Court of King Louis XIII and the lovely Queen Anne. D'Artagnan was happy, and looked forward to the day when he, too, would become a Musketeer.

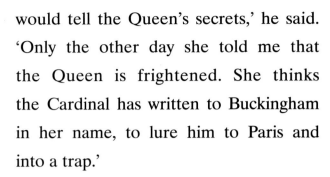

A DISAPPEARANCE

One day, while D'Artagnan was resting in his lodgings, his landlord, Monsieur Bonancieux, came upstairs to see him.

'I have heard you are a brave young man, D'Artagnan. I need help. Constance, my wife, has been kidnapped!'

'Kidnapped?' D'Artagnan asked in very great surprise.

'My wife is seamstress to the Queen,' Monsieur Bonancieux explained. 'And she is more than that. She is one of the few people the Queen can trust.'

D'Artagnan had heard a great deal about Queen Anne. Everyone knew that the King no longer loved her, and that she was lonely. The Cardinal had once cared for her, but she had rejected him. Now he plotted maliciously against her. The English Duke of Buckingham, a powerful man in the government of his own country, was in love with her. But England and France were not on friendly terms.

Monsieur Bonancieux gave a long sigh. 'I think my wife was kidnapped to see if she

would tell the Queen's secrets,' he said. 'Only the other day she told me that the Queen is frightened. She thinks the Cardinal has written to Buckingham in her name, to lure him to Paris and into a trap.'

'You think the Cardinal has taken your wife?'

'I fear so,' replied Monsieur Bonancieux. 'One of his men was seen nearby just as she was being abducted. He was a gentleman with a scar on his temple.'

D'Artagnan jumped up. 'That sounds just like the man I met in Meung!' he exclaimed.

'Please, will you help me?' Monsieur Bonancieux begged. 'You are always with the Musketeers, who are enemies of the Cardinal. I thought you and your friends would be glad to spoil his plans and help the Queen.'

'I will do what I can,' D'Artagnan promised. 'And if the man who kidnapped your wife is the man I think he is, I will be avenged for what happened to me in Meung!'

D'Artagnan hurried back to the Musketeers' headquarters. He lost no time in telling Athos,

D'Artagnan jumped up

Porthos and Aramis of the disappearance of Constance Bonancieux.

'This woman is in trouble because of her loyalty,' he told them. 'I am also anxious about the Queen's safety.'

'I have heard people say she loves our enemies, the Spanish and the English,' said Athos.

'Spain is her native country,' D'Artagnan reminded him. 'It is only natural that she should love the Spanish. As for the English, only one Englishman is involved. Buckingham, chief minister to the King of England, admires her greatly. The Cardinal and his men seem to be using this admiration in some wicked plot against the Queen.'

There was no doubt in the minds of the four friends that their true enemy was the Cardinal. If they could spoil his plans, it would be worth risking their heads. The mysterious kidnapping of Constance Bonancieux was the key to the whole intrigue. She must be found, and they would look for her together.

The four men stretched out their hands and shouted loudly, 'All for one and one for all!'

A SECRET MEETING

D'Artagnan's task was to keep watch on Monsieur Bonancieux's apartments from his own room on the upper floor. Monsieur Bonancieux had been arrested, and the Cardinal's Guards were now using his house as a trap. Anyone arriving there was taken away for questioning.

One night, D'Artagnan heard a woman's distressed cries from downstairs. Drawing his sword, he rushed down to help. The woman was Constance Bonancieux herself! She had escaped and come home, unaware that the Cardinal's men were there. Now they were trying to force her to talk. D'Artagnan's attack so surprised the guards that they ran off, leaving him with the grateful Constance Bonancieux.

'Thank you for saving me!' she cried. 'Now I must go – there is something I must do for the Queen!'

A few hours later, D'Artagnan was astonished to see her in a dark street with a Musketeer. D'Artagnan hurried to speak to them, and found the man was a stranger in a Musketeer's uniform!

The stranger turned out to be the Duke of Buckingham, and Constance Bonancieux was taking him to a secret meeting with the Queen at the Louvre. 'Please don't give us away,' she begged D'Artagnan.

Buckingham had come to Paris in response to a message. On his arrival, he had learned that this message was a trap set by the Cardinal. Now, though the Duke knew he was in danger, he refused to return to London without seeing the Queen.

D'Artagnan shook the Duke's hand. 'I will see that you reach the Louvre safely,' he promised.

At the Louvre, Madame Bonancieux led the Duke to a room, where he and the Queen could speak privately. The Queen's lovely face was pale with worry. She begged the Duke to return to England and made him promise not to see her secretly again – it was too dangerous.

'Come only as an ambassador, with guards to defend you,' she said.

'Very well,' Buckingham agreed. 'But please give me something of yours, so that I may wear it until I see you again.'

Queen Anne went into her chamber and brought out a rosewood casket. 'Here,' she said, giving the casket to the Duke. 'Take this, and go, before it is too late!'

THE CARDINAL'S PLAN

Unknown to the Queen, Cardinal Richelieu soon learned of her meeting with Buckingham. The news was brought to him by the Comte de Rochefort, the very man who had so annoyed D'Artagnan in Meung. As an ally of the Cardinal, he had placed a spy in the Queen's household.

'The Queen and Buckingham met briefly,' he told the Cardinal. 'He has already left for England.'

'Then our plan has failed,' said the Cardinal angrily.

'The Queen gave Buckingham a present before he left,' Rochefort went on. 'It was a box containing twelve diamond studs, which the King had given her as a birthday gift.'

'Well, well!' said the Cardinal, smiling slyly. 'All is not lost!'

He quickly wrote a letter, and ordered a servant to take it to London at once.

The letter said:

'Milady de Winter – Be at the first ball that Buckingham attends. He will wear on his doublet twelve diamond studs. Cut off two of these. As soon as you have them, inform me.'

King Louis XIII was the next to know that Buckingham had called on the Queen in secret, for the Cardinal told him. The King demanded to know the reason for Buckingham's visit.

'No doubt to conspire with your enemies,' replied the Cardinal.

'He came to see the Queen!' insisted the King furiously.

'I am unwilling to think so,' said the Cardinal. He was anxious to appear loyal to the Queen, while still fuelling the King's suspicions. 'However, I have been told that she cried this morning, and has spent the day writing letters.'

'I must have those letters,' cried the King, but the only ones they could find were to the Queen's brother.

The Queen was furious at the attack on her honour.

The King was remorseful. 'I had no cause to be angry with the Queen. I only hope she will forgive me,' he later said to the Cardinal.

'Perhaps if you did something to please her,' advised the Cardinal, 'her heart would soften towards you. Why not give a ball in her honour? You know how the Queen loves dancing, and it would be a chance for her to wear those beautiful diamonds you gave her for her birthday.'

The Queen was surprised and happy when she was told about the ball, and after some persuasion she did forgive her husband. Eagerly, she asked when the ball would be held.

'Cardinal Richelieu is arranging everything,' the King told her. But every day for more than a week, the Cardinal made some excuse for not setting the date.

On the eighth day the Cardinal received a letter from Milady de Winter in London. It read:

'I have them. Send money and I will bring them to Paris.'

The Cardinal knew that Milady could be there in ten to twelve  days. Content that his plans were going well, he spoke to the King about the ball.

'Today is the twentieth of September,' he said. 'The ball will take place in the Hôtel de Ville on the third of October. Do not forget, sire, to remind the Queen to wear the diamond studs!'

The Queen was delighted when Louis told her that the ball would soon take place. But her delight turned to shock and fear when he said, 'I wish you to wear your most beautiful gown and the diamond studs I gave you for your birthday.'

'When is the ball?' she asked weakly.

'The Cardinal has arranged it for twelve days from today,' replied the King.

Hearing the Cardinal mentioned, Queen Anne grew pale. 'Was it also his idea that I should wear the diamond studs?' she asked.

'What if it was?' demanded the King. 'Do I ask too much?'

The Queen shook her head. 'No, sire,' she said softly.

'Then you will appear as I ask?'

'Yes, sire.'

As soon as the King had gone, Queen Anne sank into a chair in despair. 'I am lost,' she sighed.

'I am on a secret mission for the Queen'

'The Cardinal must know everything. What am I to do?' And she began to weep.

'Don't cry, your Majesty.'

The Queen turned sharply. In the doorway stood Constance Bonancieux, who had heard every word of the King and Queen's conversation.

'Don't be afraid,' she told the Queen. 'I promise you that we will get those diamonds back in time for the ball!'

THE JOURNEY

Constance Bonancieux knew her husband would not help. The Cardinal had released him and given him money – he was now a Cardinal's man. But there was someone who could help – D'Artagnan. Knowing that he could be trusted not to betray the Queen, she told him everything that had happened.

'I will go to London at once,' he told her.

There was not a moment to be lost, so D'Artagnan asked Monsieur de Tréville if he could arrange a leave of absence for him. 'I must go to London,' he explained.

'I am on a secret mission for the Queen.'

Monsieur de Tréville looked at him sharply. 'Will anyone try to stop you?' he asked.

'The Cardinal would, if he knew,' D'Artagnan admitted.

'Then you must not go alone,' said Monsieur de Tréville. 'Athos, Porthos and Aramis will go with you. Then surely one of you at least will get to London.'

'Thank you,' said D'Artagnan gratefully.

Athos, Porthos and Aramis were as excited as D'Artagnan himself when he explained the mission.

The four adventurers left Paris at two o'clock in the morning. As long as it remained dark, they kept silent. In spite of themselves, they nervously expected ambushes on every side. As the sun rose, so did their spirits.

All went well until they arrived at Chantilly, where they stopped at an inn for breakfast. After the meal, a stranger called on Porthos to drink the Cardinal's health. Porthos agreed, if the stranger would then drink the health of the King. The stranger shouted that he would drink to no one but the Cardinal.

A bitter argument followed. Leaving Porthos to settle it, the others hurried on; Porthos would catch up with them later.

They had been travelling for several hours when they came upon some men mending the road. As they drew near, the workmen drew out concealed muskets.

'It's an ambush!' cried D'Artagnan. 'Ride on!'

They spurred their horses forward, but Aramis was wounded and could not travel far. Athos and D'Artagnan had to leave him to be looked after at a village inn.

Only D'Artagnan and Athos were left now. They rode on, and at nightfall took a room at Amiens. The night passed quietly enough, but when Athos went to pay the bill in the morning, the landlord accused him of using forged money. Four armed men rushed in. They had obviously been lying in wait.

'Ride on, D'Artagnan!' shouted Athos, his sword drawn and ready for the fight.

D'Artagnan did not need to be told twice. He galloped on and at last reached Calais, the port from which ships sailed for England. He ran onto the quay. There, a travel-weary gentleman was

asking a ship's captain to take him to England. The captain explained that the ship was ready, but the Cardinal had just issued an order – no ship was to leave the port without his permission.

'I already have the Cardinal's permission,' the gentleman said, showing the captain a paper. 'Will you take me?'

The captain agreed, but insisted that the pass had to be signed by the Port Governor. Hearing this, D'Artagnan hurried away and waited for the man to come back with the signed pass.

D'Artagnan was determined that the pass should be his, one way or the other. Naturally, the gentleman refused to give it up, and D'Artagnan had to fight him for it. At last the man gave in and handed over the precious piece of paper.

Breathing hard, D'Artagnan thrust the pass into his pocket and went to find a ship to take him to England.

THE QUEEN'S DIAMONDS

D'Artagnan boarded the ship just in time. They had scarcely left harbour when a cannon boomed out, signalling that the port was closed.

Worn out by his adventures, D'Artagnan slept while the ship sailed across the Channel. In the morning, he watched eagerly as the vessel anchored in Dover. Soon he was on his way to London.

The young Frenchman knew no English, but he had the Duke of Buckingham's name on a piece of paper. Everyone in London knew of the Duke, and D'Artagnan soon found his home.

The Duke, who remembered D'Artagnan from their meeting in the dark streets of Paris, let him in at once. His face became grave when D'Artagnan told him of the Queen's danger.

'We must return the diamond studs to her without delay!' he exclaimed. 'Louis must not find out that she gave them to me.' Taking a key from the chain he wore round his neck, the Duke unlocked the box in which the diamonds lay. As he lifted them out, he gave a startled cry: 'Two of them are missing!'

'Can you have lost them, my lord?' D'Artagnan asked anxiously.

'Never!' the Duke exclaimed. He showed D'Artagnan where the ribbon holding the two missing studs had been cut.

'Wait!' said the Duke suddenly. 'I remember now. I wore them only once, at a ball in London. Milady de Winter was there. She has never liked me, but that evening she was unusually friendly. It is she who must have taken them. She must be an agent of the Cardinal. How could I have been so foolish?'

He paced up and down, thinking hard. The King's ball was in five days' time.

If Queen Anne appeared with two of the diamond studs missing, the King's anger would be terrible, and the Cardinal would have succeeded.

Buckingham stopped suddenly and turned to D'Artagnan. 'Five days!' he exclaimed. 'That's all the time we need. I know what we must do!'

Buckingham sent for his secretary and issued an immediate order. No ships were to sail for France, for he believed Milady de Winter was still in London. Such was his importance in the government that the order was carried out without question.

Next the Duke called for his jeweller and showed him the set of diamond studs. He promised to pay the man well to make two studs exactly like them. They must be finished within two days, and made so that no one could tell the new from the old. The jeweller agreed, and hurried away to start work.

'We are not yet beaten, D'Artagnan!' cried the Duke.

Two days later the new studs were ready. The Duke and D'Artagnan examined them carefully. The jeweller had done well. It was impossible to tell that they

were not part of the original set. Now D'Artagnan could leave for France.

As his ship left Dover, he thought he saw Milady de Winter aboard one of the vessels that had been stranded there. But his ship passed so quickly that he caught little more than a glimpse of her.

Once across the Channel, D'Artagnan set off for Paris as quickly as he could.

THE BALL

Paris was full of talk about the ball. More than a week had been spent decorating the Hôtel de Ville with flowers and hundreds of candles.

The King arrived to the cheers of the watching crowds. Soon afterwards, the Queen calmly entered the ballroom. The Cardinal, looking on from behind a curtain, smiled in triumph. She was not wearing the diamond studs! He was quick to point this out to the King.

'Madame, why are you not wearing the diamond studs?' the King demanded.

The Queen noticed that the

the Queen reappeared, proudly wearing all twelve diamond studs.

'What does this mean?' demanded the King, pointing to the studs the Cardinal had given him.

The Cardinal thought quickly. 'I wished her Majesty to have them as a present,' he said. 'Not daring to offer them myself, I adopted this plan.'

'I must thank you, your Eminence,' said the Queen. Her smile showed that she understood the Cardinal's plot completely. 'I am sure these two must have cost you as much as all the others cost the King.'

D'Artagnan watched the Queen's triumph over the Cardinal. Apart from the King, the Cardinal and the Queen herself, he was the only one in the crowded ballroom who knew what had taken place.

Later, the Queen sent for him. She thanked him, and gave him a diamond ring. D'Artagnan returned to the ball feeling well contented. He was in favour with the King and Monsieur de Tréville, and he had helped his Queen when she most needed it. Above all, he had gained the friendship of three brave men, Athos, Porthos and Aramis. One day he, too, would be a Musketeer, just like them.

Cardinal was watching her. 'Sire,' she replied, 'I was afraid they would come to harm in this crowd. But I will do as you ask, and send for them.'

While the Queen waited with her ladies in a side room, the Cardinal gave the King the box containing the two studs Milady de Winter had stolen from Buckingham.

'Ask the Queen where these have come from,' he suggested.

But his triumph turned to rage when

Gulliver's Travels

by Jonathan Swift
illustrated by Nick Harris

My Arrival in a Strange Land

I was for some years a physician in London, but my business had begun to fail. So, having consulted with my wife, I decided to go to sea. On May 4th, 1699, I said goodbye to my family and set sail from Bristol as a ship's doctor bound for the South Seas.

All went well for the first few weeks. Then there was a bad storm and the ship was wrecked. Six of the crew, of whom I was one, got into a little boat and began to row to an island nearby. Suddenly a huge wave upset the boat, and all the other men were lost. Only I, Lemuel Gulliver, was left.

I swam as long as I could. At last, just as I could swim no more, my feet touched the bottom. I waded to the shore, where there was no sign of houses or people.

I walked about half a mile further, but still saw no one. Tired out, I lay down on the short, soft grass and went to sleep.

When I woke up it was daylight. I lay still for a moment, wondering where I was, then tried to get up. I could not move my arms or my legs or my head! I was tied to the ground! There was a buzzing noise near me, but I could not see what was making it.

I… set sail from Bristol

Suddenly I felt something moving on my left leg. It walked up me and stopped close by my chin. I looked down as well as I could (for my hair was tied to the ground) and saw a tiny man, less than six inches high, with a bow and arrow in his hand. Then many more of these little men started to run all over me. I was so surprised that I roared loudly. They ran back in fright and fell over one another trying to get away.

I managed to break the strings that tied my left arm to the ground, and pulled some of my hair loose so that I could move my head. This made the little men even more afraid, and they shot arrows at me. Some fell on my hands and some on my face, pricking me like needles and making my skin sore.

The little men stood around at a distance, watching me. After a while, when they saw that I was not going to hurt them, they cut some of the strings that bound me. This at least allowed me to move my head more freely.

Now I could see that they had built a little platform beside my head so that they could talk to me. A well-dressed gentleman climbed

up and began to speak to me. He spoke for some time, but I could not understand him, and I began to grow very hungry. I pointed to my mouth and pretended to chew. He seemed to understand and at once sent men to bring me food and drink.

Ladders were put against my sides, and over a hundred of the little men climbed up, bringing baskets of meat and bread. Each piece of meat was the size of one small piece of mince, so I had to keep asking for more. The loaves were so tiny that I ate three at a time.

I drank a whole barrel of their wine at a gulp, which was not difficult to do, as the barrel held hardly half a pint. They kept looking at each other as if they could not believe it was possible to drink so much, but they brought me some more wine, which I drank as well.

I made signs to let them know I would not try to escape, and they loosened the strings so that I could turn on my side.

They also put some ointment on my face and hands, which took away the soreness their arrows had caused.

Then I fell asleep again.

THE EMPEROR

When I woke up I found myself on a kind of platform with wheels. It was moving towards the capital city of these tiny people, about half a mile away. Fifteen hundred large horses, each about as big as my hand, were pulling me along.

I later found out that it had taken five hundred carpenters and engineers to make this platform, and nine hundred men to put me onto it while I was still asleep.

For some time I did not know what had wakened me. I was told later, however, that some of the young people had climbed onto the platform and walked very softly up to my face. One of them, an officer in the guards, put the sharp end of his spear up into my nose, which tickled my nose like a straw and made me sneeze, waking me up.

We marched for the remainder of that day and rested at night. Five hundred guards were put on each side of me, ready to shoot me if I tried to escape.

At last we arrived at the capital. The platform to which I was tied stopped outside a temple that was no longer used.

Since this was the largest building in the whole country, the Emperor had planned that I should live there. The door was just big enough for me to creep through. Once inside, I could only lie down.

The little men, however, would not let me go free. They put nearly a hundred of their tiny chains around my left leg so that, although I could stand up, I could not move very far.

When this was done, the Emperor visited me. He carried a sword about as big as one of our darning needles, to defend himself if I should break loose. He was much taller than the rest of his court, and he wore a gold helmet with a plume on the crest.

I tried to answer the Emperor when he spoke to me, but he could not understand any of the languages I speak. Soon he went away to decide whether to have me killed, for I would cost a great deal to feed, and might be dangerous.

Soon afterwards, a great crowd of the tiny people came to see me. Some of the men shot arrows at me, and one just missed my eye. The guards tied these men up and gave them to me to punish.

I put five of them in my pocket and pretended I was going to eat the other one, who was very frightened. Then I took out my penknife and cut the cords that bound him, and set him on the ground. I treated the other five in the same way, taking them out of my pocket one by one; everyone was very surprised to see me treat them so gently.

Two of the guards went to the Emperor to tell him what I had done. He decided that since I had been kind to his people, he would not have me killed. He ordered people who lived close to the town to bring me six cows and forty sheep every day, and wine to drink. This was only just enough for me, since everything was so tiny.

Three hundred tailors were told to make clothes for me, and six hundred little people were to look after me. They were to live in tents outside the temple to make it easier for them to get to me.

Lastly, six men were to teach me their language.

I AM SEARCHED

Three weeks later, I was able to understand and talk to the little men. The first thing I asked for was my freedom. The Emperor said that they must first see if I was carrying anything that could be a danger to his people, and so I would have to be searched.

Two men came to look through my pockets, and wrote down everything they found. They gave me a new name – the Great Man Mountain.

In my pockets they found:

A handkerchief, which they thought was like a carpet.

A snuffbox, which they called a chest filled with dust. It made them sneeze.

A notebook, in which they recognised very large handwriting.

A comb. They knew what this was for, but said it looked like the railings around the Emperor's palace.

A knife, *a razor* and *a pair of pistols*. All these things were new to them, and they could not think what they were for.

A watch. They thought it must be a god that I worshipped, because I told them I always looked at it before I did anything.

A purse. They called this a net large enough for a fisherman, but they knew I used it as a purse. They were very surprised at the size of the gold pieces in it.

When the two little men had finished looking in my pockets, they looked at my belt. They wrote down that I had a sword as long as five men and a pouch with two pockets. One of these pockets held black powder, the other very heavy, round balls.

They took their list to the Emperor, who asked me to take out my sword and put it carefully on the ground. Then he asked me what my pistols were for. I told him not to be afraid, and I fired one in the air.

Everyone fell down in fright except the Emperor, although he, too, went very white. He made me give up my pistols at once. I did so, telling him that the black powder must be kept away from fire because it was very dangerous.

All my things were put away in the Emperor's storeroom, except for my eyeglasses, which were in a pocket the men had not found.

Slowly the Emperor and his people

came to understand that they were in no danger from me. From time to time some of them would dance on my hand, and the boys and girls liked to play hide-and-seek in my hair as I lay on the ground. Even the horses stopped being afraid of me, and horses and riders would take turns to leap over my hand as I held it on the ground.

I AM SET FREE

One day some people came to tell the Emperor that they had found a huge, black object lying on the ground, and they thought it might belong to the Great Man Mountain. It was my hat, which I thought I had lost at sea! To bring it to me, they made two holes in the brim and fastened cords from the hat to the harnesses of five horses. It was then dragged along the ground. This did not do it much good!

Another time the Emperor asked me to stand with my legs apart so that his army could march between them. There were three thousand foot soldiers and one thousand horsemen, marching with drums beating and flags flying.

I asked once more to be set free, and at last the Emperor agreed, as long as I would obey his rules.

I had always wanted to see the capital city, and now that I was free the Emperor said I could. All the people were told to stay in their houses in case I walked on them. So they crowded to their windows to see me as I stepped over the wall into the city where the Emperor's palace stood.

It was really magnificent, like a big doll's house. I lay down to look inside and the Empress came to the window, smiling, and gave me her hand to kiss.

Soon after I was set free, one of the country's great men came to see me. We had a long talk, and I learned many things.

I had thought the island, which was called Lilliput, was a peaceful and happy one, but he told me this was not so.

'You may have seen,' he said, 'that some of us wear high heels and some wear low heels on our shoes. The Emperor will let only people wearing low heels work for him, and those who like high heels feel that this is wrong. Because of this there are many quarrels among the Lilliputians.'

Then he told me of a much bigger

I stepped over the wall into the city

danger that was about to befall his country. 'There is an island close by called Blefuscu, and the people there are going to attack us.'

'Why?' I asked him.

'It all began a long, long time ago,' he replied. 'When our Emperor's great-grandfather was a little boy, he cut his finger one morning as he took the top off his egg. Up till then everyone had cut off the big end of the egg. After that, however, the ruler of those times said that everyone must cut off the small end. Those who would not obey had to leave Lilliput. They went to Blefuscu and called themselves the Big-Endians. Now they are coming to make war on Lilliput, and the Emperor wants you to help us.'

PEACE IS RESTORED

I said I would help the people of Lilliput in any way I could, for they had been very kind to me.

I knew that the Big-Endians had about fifty war ships lying at anchor, and I planned to seize them.

I fixed fifty hooks to fifty lengths of cord, then set off for Blefuscu. There was only about half a mile of sea between the islands, and I could wade most of the way.

The enemy took fright when they saw me, and leapt out of their ships and swam to shore. I then fastened a hook to the prow of each ship, and tied all the cords together at the end. While I was doing this, the Big-Endians shot thousands of tiny arrows at me. I was afraid one would go in my eye, so I put on my glasses.

After I had cut the anchor cables, I took up the knotted end of the cords to which my hooks were tied, and set off back to Lilliput with fifty of the enemy's largest ships.

The Emperor was so pleased with me that he made me a nardac, which is something like a duke in my own land. He now wanted me to seize the rest of the enemy's ships, so that he could be Emperor of the Big-Endians as well as Lilliput. I would not carry out the Emperor's wishes, as I did not think it would be right to do so. This made the Emperor angry with me.

Soon after this, some of the Big-Endians came to make peace

I was dangerous. They all asked the Emperor to have me put to death as an enemy of Lilliput.

The Emperor refused to have me put to death, because I had helped him. He thought that the best way to punish me would be to put out my eyes.

One of the great men was my friend. He came in secret to tell me what the Emperor had said, so that I could save myself. When I heard what he had to say, I felt that the time had come for me to leave Lilliput.

I RETURN HOME

I went down to the shore and took one of the Emperor's ships. I put my clothes in it so that they would not get wet, and pulled it after me as I swam across to Blefuscu.

The Emperor of Blefuscu was pleased to see me, and so were all his people. They were kind to me, and I liked them, but I did not want to spend the rest of my life there.

One day I saw, out at sea, a full-sized

with the Lilliputians. When they saw me again, they asked me to come to Blefuscu. I said that I would, which made the Emperor even more angry with me. His chief admiral was displeased with me, too, not only because I had defeated the Big-Endian navy (which he could not do), but also because I had been made a nardac.

There were others amongst the Emperor's great men who did not like me, some of them because I ate so much of their food, and some who thought boat floating upside down. I asked the Emperor for some ships and men to help me bring it to shore, so that I could sail home in it.

It took two thousand of the tiny men to help me turn the boat the right way up once it was ashore. Then I had to get ready for the long journey home.

The thickest linen these people had was much thinner than that of our finest handkerchiefs, so thirteen thicknesses were put together to make two sails for me. It took five hundred workmen to make them! I made ropes and cables by twisting together thirty of the thickest and strongest of their ropes. I made oars and masts with the help of the Emperor's ship-carpenters. A large, heavy stone that I found would serve as an anchor.

When all was ready, I stored food on board, and also live cows and bulls and sheep, which I wanted to show my family. I would have liked to take some of the little people with me, but the Emperor would not allow me to.

It took about a month to complete the preparations. When all was ready I set off, and two days later I saw a big ship, whose captain took me on board. He did not believe my story until he saw the live cows and sheep, which were in my pocket.

When at last I got home, my wife and children were very happy to see me again and to hear all my adventures. As for the cows and sheep, I put them to eat grass in a park close by my house, at Greenwich in London. There they thrived, and they have since increased greatly in number!

ANOTHER ADVENTURE

I stayed at home for just two months. Then the yearning for travel overtook me again, and I set sail once more aboard a merchant ship called the *Adventure*.

The first part of our voyage was pleasant, with nothing to trouble us. But one day a bad storm blew up, and we were driven hundreds of miles out of our way.

We were lost. There was plenty of food on board, but not nearly enough water. So when the lookout in the topmast spotted land, the captain sent several of us ashore to get water.

I ran away as fast as I could and climbed a steep hill. From there I could see the surrounding country.

I could not believe my eyes! The grass was nearly as tall as a house, with corn towering above it as high as a church steeple!

I walked along what I thought was a main road, but which I found out later was just a footpath. At last I came to a stile. Each step in this stile was like a high wall to me, and I could not climb it.

As I was looking for a gap in the huge hedge, I saw another enormous man. I was very frightened, and ran to hide in the corn.

He called out in a voice that sounded to me like thunder, and seven other giants came towards him. They carried scythes, each as big as six of our own.

I grew even more frightened. Where could I hide? I ran to and fro to keep out of their way, but they moved too fast for me to escape.

At last, just as one was about to step on me, I called out 'Stop!' as loudly as I could. The man looked down and picked me up, holding me tightly in case I should bite him. I tried to let him know, by groaning and turning my head from

When we landed there was no sign of a river or spring, nor of any inhabitants. The other men kept to the shore, while I walked inland. The country seemed barren and rocky, with no water to be seen, and so I turned back.

From where I stood, I could see our ship's boat with all the men on board, rowing as quickly as they could back to the ship. They had left me behind! Then I saw why. There was a huge, manlike creature chasing them, taking great strides through the sea.

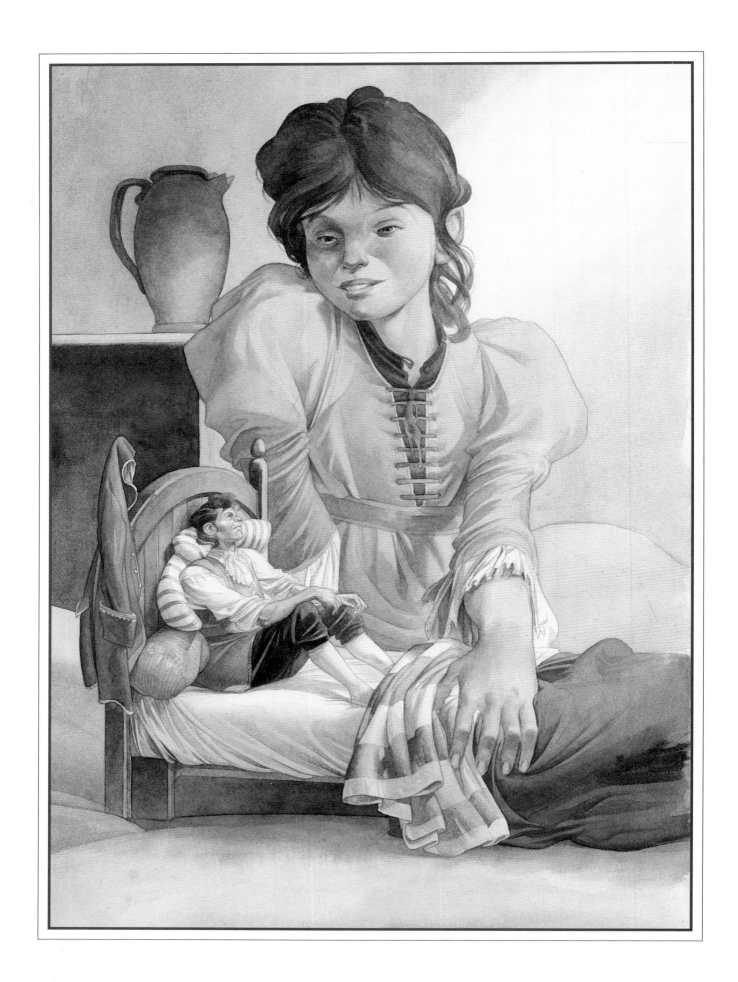

This girl was very good to me

side to side, how much he was hurting me. He seemed to understand, and eased his grip. Then he took me to his master to show him what he had found. This man was a farmer, and the same man I had seen at first in the field.

The farmer wrapped me in his handkerchief and took me back to his farm. His wife screamed and ran away when she saw me, just as my wife does when she sees a mouse!

Then the three children came to have a look at me. They were just going to have their dinner, and they put me on the table, where they could see me as they ate. It was like being on the roof of a house. I kept as far as I could from the edge, for fear of falling.

The farmer's wife gave me some crumbs of bread and minced up some meat for me. I took out my knife and fork and started to eat, which delighted them. The farmer's wife filled her smallest cup (it was as big as a bucket) with cider for me, but I could not drink it all!

Then in came the nurse with the baby. He wanted me as a plaything. When they gave me to him, he put my head in his mouth. I roared so

loudly that the baby was frightened and dropped me. I would have been killed if his mother had not caught me in her apron.

Later on, the daughter of the house made a bed for me in the baby's cradle. This girl was very good to me. She was nine years old and small for her age in that country, since she was only forty feet tall! She called me Grildrig, which meant 'Little Man', and taught me to speak their language. I liked her very much.

LIFE AMONG THE GIANTS

As soon as the people who lived round about heard of me, they came to have a look at me. One of them told the farmer that he should take me to town next market day and make people pay to see me.

So on the next market day, the farmer put me into a little box and set off with me. His little girl came with us to look after me. She was very worried in case some harm should come to me, and she put a little quilt in the box to make me more comfortable.

I was grateful for her company, and I called her my nurse.

As soon as we arrived in town, the farmer took me to an inn he frequented. There I was placed on a table, and people were invited in to see me.

I did all the funny tricks I could think of: I stood on my head, I hopped about and I danced. I picked up a thimble, which my nurse had given me for a cup, and I drank everyone's health.

The spectators were delighted, and the room filled nearly to bursting with all those who wanted to watch me.

The farmer made a great deal of money from showing me, and he decided to take me to other towns. So we travelled round the country, and I was shown in many towns and villages. After several weeks, we came to the capital city, where the royal family lived.

The Queen liked me so much that she bought me from the farmer. I begged her to let my nurse stay with me, and she agreed. The farmer gave his consent as well, and the little girl could barely hide her joy.

The Queen had a little room made for me, with a roof that lifted up and furniture that was just the right size for me. To them it was a small box, which could be attached to a belt for carrying. The Queen had a set of silver cups, saucers and plates made for me, too. It was like a doll's tea set to her!

I always had my meals at a little table on the Queen's table, just at her elbow. It upset me to see the way the Queen ate. She would put a piece of bread as big as two of our loaves in her mouth at one go! Her dinner knife was taller than me, and I thought it looked very dangerous.

Every Wednesday, which was their Sunday, the King came to have dinner with us. He asked me many questions about England. He wanted to know in what ways we were different from the people in his own country of Brobdingnag.

The only member of court I did not get along with was the Queen's dwarf. He was five times as tall as me – about thirty feet – but this was small to his people. The King was twice as tall as he was! He was jealous because the Queen seemed to like me better than him, and he played tricks on me. Once he dropped me in a jug of cream. I swam to the side, and my

in through an open window. They were as big as our pigeons, with stings as long as my thumb and sharp as needles! As they flew about my head and face, I managed to fight them off with my dagger.

On another day, a monkey came into my room and picked me up. I think he took me for a baby monkey, for he stroked my face gently as he held me. Suddenly there was a noise at the door, and he leapt through the window and up to the roof, carrying me with him. The servants had to get ladders and climb up in order to drive the monkey away and bring me down.

AN EVENTFUL JOURNEY

One day when the King and I were talking, I said I could teach him to make gunpowder so that he could win a lot of wars. The King, however, was horrified when I explained to him how gunpowder works, and described the destruction that guns can cause. He refused and said that he would rather lose half his kingdom than use such weapons.

nurse fished me out. The Queen became so cross with the dwarf that she finally sent him away.

I was pleased when they made a little boat for me and put it in a tub of water so that I could row about. Sometimes they put a sail on the boat. Then the Queen and her women would make a breeze for me with their fans. It was great fun for me.

Sometimes, however, life in Brobdingnag was no fun at all! Once, when I was eating breakfast, about twenty wasps swarmed

Soon after this the King and Queen and their servants set off on a long journey to another part of Brobdingnag. I went with them in my box. They fixed up a hammock in it so that I should not feel the bumps so much as we went along.

My nurse came too, but she got a bad cold on the way. When at last we came to a stop, she had to rest for a few days.

I knew we were near the sea, and I longed to see it again. Since my nurse was confined to her bed, one of the Queen's pages was told to take me to the seashore.

My nurse did not want to let me go, almost as if she had some foreboding of what was to happen. But at last, in floods of tears and with many warnings to the page to be careful, she consented.

I was put into my box, and the boy carried me to the rocky coast. I lay in my hammock, looking out at the sea and feeling sad. When would I see my home again?

After some time the page went off to look for birds' eggs, and I fell asleep.

I awoke suddenly with a jolt. There was a loud swishing noise above me, and my box seemed to be moving upwards very fast. I called out several times, but no one answered.

Then I guessed what had happened. A very large bird, perhaps an eagle, had swooped down and picked up my box in his beak. I was flying through the air!

Soon there came a loud squawking, as if the eagle were fighting, and all at once I was falling, faster and faster. At last my box stopped with a great *splash*!

THE VOYAGE HOME

After a moment I stopped trembling and looked out of the window. I was at sea!

I pulled open a little trap door in the roof of my box to let in some fresh air. Then I called for help, but no one heard me. How I wished my nurse was with me!

I took out my handkerchief and tied it to my walking stick. Then I stood on a chair and pushed this flag through the little trap door, waving it to and fro and calling for help again. No one came, and I gave myself up for lost.

I sat without hope for a long time. Then, suddenly, I realised that my box was being pulled along.

Once more I pushed my flag out of the trap door and called loudly for help. This time, to my great joy, someone answered – in English! He told me I was safe, and that my box was tied to the side of his ship.

Someone was sent to cut a hole in the box and, with the help of a ladder and many willing hands, I was pulled up onto the deck. It was an English ship, with English sailors – not giants, not little men, but people the same size as me!

When I told them my story, the captain and his crew did not believe me. They thought I had been shut up in the box because I had done something very bad. I was not surprised, so I showed them a gold ring the Queen had given me – it was so big I wore it round my neck like a collar. And I gave the captain a giant's tooth which a Brobdingnagian dentist had taken out. It was as big as a wine bottle!

At last the men believed me. The captain said he would take me back to England, and we set sail for home.

Many weeks later, when I came on land again, the houses and people all looked so small compared to those of Brobdingnag that, for a moment, I thought I must be in Lilliput once more.

When my wife heard what I had been through, she said I must never go to sea again. For myself, I was glad to be back at home with my family. I had had quite enough adventure for some time!

TREASURE ISLAND

by Robert Louis Stevenson
illustrated by David Frankland

THE SEA-CHEST

I remember, as if it were yesterday, the old seaman who came to live at our inn. He was tall, with a black pigtail that hung down to his shoulder, and he had a scar across one cheek. His name was Billy Bones, and when he was drunk, as he often was, we were all afraid of him. He never talked to the sailors who called at the inn, and he paid me fourpence a month to warn him if I should ever see a sailor with one leg.

Dr Livesey warned Billy Bones that rum would kill him, but he didn't care to change his ways. When he lay weak and helpless in his bed, he told me dreadful stories of walking the plank, storms at sea and the wicked deeds of men.

He had been the mate on the pirate ship of Captain Flint. When the Captain was dying, he gave Billy Bones a map that showed where his treasure was buried. Since that day, the rest of Flint's old crew had been trying to get hold of the map. It was hidden in Billy Bones' sea-chest.

One frosty afternoon an old blind seaman, Blind Pew, called at the inn and asked for Billy Bones. He gripped Billy's hand as he left, and something passed from his hand to Billy's.

His name was Billy Bones

Fear filled Billy's eyes when he saw what it was. 'The black spot!' he cried. 'Jim Hawkins, listen to me. This black spot means that my old shipmates are coming to get me. They're after my map, Jim! They'll kill me!' He sprang up as he spoke, and the strain and shock must have been too much. He fell dead at my feet.

Billy Bones died without paying his bills. My mother and I took some money from his sea-chest, to pay what he owed. There was also a bundle of papers, which I took for safekeeping.

That night a gang of ruffians broke into our inn. My mother and I hid and watched as they searched Billy Bones' sea-chest. They took the remaining money, but they seemed to be looking for something else. Unable to find it, they shouted and raged. I realised that they were after the bundle of papers in my pocket.

I went to Dr Livesey and his friend Squire Trelawney and told them the whole story. When we opened the bundle we found Captain Flint's treasure map.

'Flint was the most bloodthirsty pirate that ever sailed,' the Squire cried. 'I'll fit out a ship in Bristol!

Livesey, you'll be ship's doctor, and Jim Hawkins, you'll be cabin boy. We'll have the best ship in England – and we'll have that treasure!'

So it was that Squire Trelawney bought the *Hispaniola* and prepared her for the voyage. He took on a sailor named Long John Silver as ship's cook. Silver's left leg was cut off close by the hip, and under his left arm he carried a crutch. He was very tall and strong. Silver helped the Squire to assemble a tough, hard-working crew, and soon the *Hispaniola* was ready to sail.

THE VOYAGE

We set sail under our captain, Captain Smollett. The coxswain, Israel Hands, was an able man, and Long John Silver was a fine cook. We all worked well and willingly, and I often heard the crew singing as they toiled. The song was one I'd heard from old Billy Bones:

'Fifteen men on the Dead Man's Chest –
Yo-ho-ho and a bottle of rum!'

I passed many spare moments in Silver's shining galley. His parrot,

Captain Flint, named after the pirate, swung in its cage and screeched, 'Pieces of eight! Pieces of eight!' all day long.

Silver was interesting company, full of gripping yarns of his other voyages and adventures. He was well liked by all, and the men looked up to him as a leader.

We kept a barrel of apples on deck, for the men to help themselves. One evening I went to the barrel and, finding it nearly empty, climbed inside to get an apple from the bottom. There I sat, quietly rocked by the sea.

Someone sat down on the deck, leaned against the barrel and started to speak. The words I overheard made my blood run cold. Israel Hands and Silver were planning to take over the ship once we had found the treasure. They had agreed to kill the Captain and anyone who would not fall in with them! I could not believe my ears.

Suddenly someone shouted 'Land-ho!' As the men all ran to catch the first sight of land, I jumped out of the barrel and ran to the safety of my friends.

Captain Smollett was telling the crew about the island. Long John Silver said that he'd been there before when his ship had put in for water. I looked at his smiling face and shuddered. I now knew that Silver was more than a cheerful ship's cook. He was also a ruthless pirate!

As soon as I could, I told the Captain, the Squire and the Doctor what I had heard. They decided we were safe until the treasure was found. When we were ready we would surprise the pirates, and hope to catch them unprepared.

We now lay off Treasure Island, a gloomy, forbidding place. The air was hot and still, and the men were restless.

Captain Smollett gave leave for them to go ashore, which raised their spirits. I believe they thought they would stumble on treasure as soon as they landed!

Long John Silver was in charge of the two boats taking thirteen men ashore. I knew I should not be needed on board and decided to go ashore, too.

MY SHORE ADVENTURE BEGINS

I ran up the beach into the woods, glad to be free and alone. As I sat hidden in the bushes, I heard voices and moved nearer to catch the words. Silver was bullying a sailor to join the pirates. When the sailor refused, Silver plunged his dagger into the man and left him lying dead in the forest.

Fearing for my life, I ran, not caring where. At the foot of a hill my eye was caught by a movement, but I could not tell if it was a man or an animal. I felt I could not face this new danger, so I began to run towards the shore.

But the creature was fast and, darting from tree to tree, he came closer. I could see now that it was a man, but so wild and strange that I was afraid. As he neared me he threw himself down and held up his hands, as if begging for mercy.

I had never seen such a ragged creature. He was dressed in a patchwork of tattered cloth, and his blue eyes looked startling in a face burnt black by the sun. 'Who are you?' I asked.

'I'm poor Ben Gunn, I am,' he answered. 'It's three years since I spoke to anyone.' Babbling in a high, squeaky voice, he told me he was rich. Sometimes he spoke sense, and sometimes his words had no meaning. I felt he might be crazy after being alone for so long.

He said that he'd been on Captain Flint's pirate ship, and that three years before he had come back with some seamen to look for Flint's treasure. When they could not find it, the sailors went off, leaving him alone on the island. When he'd seen our ship, he'd thought that Flint had returned.

I told him that Flint was dead, but some of Flint's old shipmates were among our crew. When I spoke of Silver, his face filled with terror. I told him we should have to fight the pirates, and he promised to help us if we would take him back with us.

Our talk was interrupted by gunfire. Running towards the sound we came upon a high wooden fence that ran round a cleared space in the forest. The Union Jack flew from a log house in the clearing.

I knew that my friends must have left the ship and were defending themselves in the log house. The battle with the pirates had begun! The *Hispaniola* lay in the inlet with the Jolly Roger at her mast. On the beach a group of drunken sailors lolled on the sand.

I parted from Ben Gunn and climbed the stockade to join my friends in the log house. They were delighted to see me, and Dr Livesey told me what had happened after I left the ship.

The Captain had decided it was time to fight it out with the pirates. He knew of the log house from Flint's map, so he and the Squire and Dr Livesey had loaded a small boat with food and ammunition and, with the rest of the *Hispaniola*'s faithful crew, made a dash for the shore.

There was a small group of pirates still on board the ship. When they saw what was happening, they had fired on the little boat, and it had sunk in shallow water. The Squire's party had waded ashore, but lost half the stores and gunpowder.

The Doctor was sure the pirates would soon give up the fight. He said they would get ill from too much rum, and with disease from their swampy campsite.

I told my friends of my meeting with Ben Gunn. Dr Livesey wanted to know all about him, for we clearly needed help. We had little food, and the pirates could soon starve us out. I was worn out at the end of a hard day, and soon fell asleep.

THE ATTACK

In the morning I awoke to the sound of voices. Long John Silver himself was approaching the stockade, carrying a white flag. Captain Smollett, suspecting a trick, ordered us to be ready to fire.

Silver said he had come to make terms to end the fighting, and he was allowed into the stockade. He told the Captain that the pirates intended to get the treasure. In exchange for the treasure map, he offered to take us to a safe place off the island.

Captain Smollett was not a man to make terms with pirates. Angrily, he told Silver that he and the pirates were done for. Without the map, they had no hope of finding the treasure. And with or without the treasure, not one of them could plot a course to sail the ship home. He ordered Silver to leave. Fury blazed in Silver's eyes, and with curses and threats, he disappeared into the wood.

We now prepared for the coming attack, and sat and waited in the baking heat. All at once musket shots hit the log house, and pirates leapt from the woods and climbed the stockade. Shouts and groans, shots and flashes filled the air.

I grabbed a cutlass and dashed outside to join the fight. In moments we had fought the pirates back. Those who were not killed or injured scurried to the woods.

Two of our men had been lost, and the Captain was badly injured. We were certain there would be a second attack, so we waited. But all was quiet.

In the lull I saw Dr Livesey quietly leave the stockade. I guessed he was going to Ben Gunn. Still no attack came, and I grew weary of waiting. The heat, the blood and the dust made me restless, and I longed to get away to a cool, fresh place. I knew the Captain would never let me go, so when no one was looking I put two pistols in my pocket and slipped out.

I ran to the shore and felt the cool wind. The surf tossed its foam along the beach. Climbing a hill, I could look down on the calm inlet where the *Hispaniola* lay. In a little boat beside her, I could make out Long John Silver, talking with two men on the ship. No words reached me, but the screeching of Silver's parrot was carried on the wind.

I could look down on the calm inlet

About sundown, Silver shoved off for shore and the other two men went below deck. I was sure that if the pirates could not find the treasure they would sail away without us. A plan began to grow in my mind.

If I could get to the *Hispaniola*, I could cut her anchor ropes. She would drift away to another part of the shore, and the pirates would be unable to escape.

Ben Gunn had told me that he had made a boat and hidden it near the shore. I searched in the bushes and, to my joy, found the little boat. It was very flimsy, and I hoped it would hold me.

With darkness, fog crept into the inlet. It was a perfect night for my plan. I pushed away from the shore and drifted silently towards the *Hispaniola*.

MY SEA ADVENTURE BEGINS

As I came alongside the ship I could hear loud, drunken voices. Israel Hands was shouting at another man. They were very angry, and both the worse for rum. On the shore I could see the glow of the fire in the pirates' camp. Someone there was singing the song I'd heard so often before:

'Fifteen men on the Dead Man's Chest –
Yo-ho-ho and a bottle of rum!
Drink and the devil had done for the rest –
Yo-ho-ho and a bottle of rum!'

Strand by strand, I cut the anchor rope, and the ship began to swing and slide away to the open sea. As she slid past me, I could see into the cabin. Israel Hands and the ship's watchman were fighting.

They were too busy to feel the movement of the ship. I lay flat in my little boat, praying that I should not be seen.

For hours, as the sea grew rough again, I was tossed on the waves. I must have slept, for it was daylight when I awoke. My boat had drifted along the coast, but I could see no landing place under the rocky cliffs. I could only let my boat drift on and hope to find a sandy shore.

As I rounded a headland, the sight before me made me forget my cares. No more than half a mile away lay the *Hispaniola*! Her sails were set, but by the way she turned and drifted, it was clear no one was steering her. If the pirates were drunk and I could get aboard, I might be able to capture the ship!

I paddled fast, but with the wind filling her sails, the *Hispaniola* kept her lead. At last the breeze fell and I had my chance. I came alongside and leapt aboard. The wind took her sails, and she rushed down on a wave and sank my little boat. I had no way of escape now.

I moved quietly on the bloodstained deck, and at length I saw two pirates. One was dead. The other was Israel Hands, wounded and 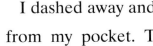 unable to stand. He begged for brandy to ease his pain, and I went below into the wrecked cabin to find some. He seemed stronger after a drink.

I agreed to give Hands food and to patch up his wounds, if he would tell me how to steer the ship into a safe harbour. For the time being, we needed each other. But I did not trust him.

He asked me to fetch some wine from the cabin, and when he thought I had gone below, he staggered across the deck and picked up a knife he had hidden in his jacket. This was all I needed to know. I was certain he meant to kill me as soon as we brought the ship ashore.

IN THE ENEMY'S CAMP

The beaching was difficult and took all my care, so I was too busy to keep watch on Hands all the time. Suddenly I sensed danger. Sure enough, when I looked round, Hands was coming towards me, a dagger in his right hand.

I dashed away and pulled a pistol from my pocket. Turning, I took aim and fired. But there was no flash, no sound. The powder was wet with seawater.

The ship gave a sudden lurch as she hit the shore, and we were both thrown off our feet. Before Hands could stand again, I had climbed the mast. Safe for the moment, I sat in the rigging and put dry powder in my pistols. Hands was slowly coming up the mast after me, his dagger between his teeth.

'One more step, Mr Hands,' I called, 'and I'll blow your brains out!' He stopped and in a flash flung his dagger. I felt a sharp pain and found myself pinned to the mast by the shoulder. The sudden pain and shock made me fire both my pistols. With a cry, Israel Hands fell headfirst into the water.

I felt sick and faint and shut my eyes until I became calm. When I had freed myself, I found that the wound was not very deep, in spite of the blood that ran down my arm. In the cabin I found bandages to bind up my wound.

It was now sunset, and I waded ashore. All I wanted was to be back with my friends. I hoped that the capture of the *Hispaniola* would

be enough for them to forgive me for having left them.

The moon helped me to find my way to the stockade. I walked carefully and silently and dropped over the fence. There was no sound. The man on watch had not heard me. I crept to the log house and stepped inside.

Suddenly a shrill voice rang out in the darkness: 'Pieces of eight! Pieces of eight! Pieces of eight!' Silver's parrot!

Instead of finding my friends, I had come face to face with the pirates – and capture. By the light of a flaming torch, I saw Silver and the five men who were still alive.

There was no sign of my friends, and my first thought was that they had all been killed. But I soon learned that this was not so.

While I had been away, Dr Livesey had gone to the pirates and told them that, because the ship had gone, he and his party had given up the search for treasure. The log house and everything in it, even the treasure map, was handed over to the pirates and my friends had walked out into the woods.

This news puzzled me. I could

not understand why they had given up without a fight.

Long John Silver was still the pirate leader, but he seemed less cheerful than before. It was clear that the men did not obey him willingly. If they should pick a new leader, Silver knew that they would kill him. His only hope of being saved was to be on Captain Smollett's side.

He promised to protect me from the pirates, if I would put in a good word for him with the Captain. But if the pirates guessed he had changed sides, I knew

they would finish us both. Our lives depended on keeping our plan secret.

The next morning Dr Livesey came to the log house to see to the sick and wounded. He was surprised to see me with the pirates, but he said nothing. He went on his rounds, giving out medicine and dressing wounds. When he had finished, he asked to speak to me alone.

The Doctor spoke harshly to me at first, telling me it was cowardly to have joined the pirates. But when I told him of all that had happened to me, his view changed.

When he heard that the *Hispaniola* was safe, the Doctor was amazed. I told him of Silver's danger, and he agreed to take him home with us if Silver would keep me safe. We were in a tight corner, and it looked as if there was little hope of getting out of it. At last the Doctor shook my hand and said he was off to get help.

The pirates were growing restless to go out and find the treasure. But there was a question in Silver's mind – why had the treasure map been given to him? He knew there must be a trick, and he dared not let the pirates guess his thoughts.

We set out to find Captain Flint's treasure

The Treasure Hunt

With picks and shovels, we set out to find Captain Flint's treasure. The men were armed to the teeth. As I was a prisoner, I had a rope tied round my waist. Silver held the other end. In spite of his promise to keep me safe, I did not trust him.

As we went, the men talked about the chart. On the back of it was written:

'Tall tree, Spy-glass Shoulder,
    bearing a point to the N. of N.N.E.
Skeleton Island E.S.E. and by E.
    Ten feet.'

So we were looking for a tall tree on a hill. The men were in high spirits, and Silver and I could not keep up with them.

Suddenly there was a shout from one of the men. The others ran towards him, full of hope. But it was not treasure he had found. At the foot of the tree lay a human skeleton.

The men looked down in horror. The few rags of clothing that hung on the bones showed that the man had been a sailor. The skeleton was stretched out straight, the feet pointing one way and the arms, raised above the head, pointing in the opposite direction.

'This here's one of Flint's little jokes!' cried Silver. 'These bones point E.S.E. and by E. This is one of the men he killed, and he's laid him here to point the way!'

The men felt a chill in their hearts, for they had all lived in fear of Flint. 'But he's dead,' said one of them.

'Aye, sure enough, he's dead and gone below,' said another pirate. 'But if ever a ghost walked, it would be Flint's.'

'Aye,' said a third man. 'I tell you, I don't like to hear "Fifteen Men" sung now, for it was the only song he ever sang.'

Silver put an end to their talk and we moved on, but now the men spoke softly and kept together. Just the thought of Flint was enough to fill them with terror.

At the top of the hill we rested. In whispers, the men still talked of Flint.

'Ah, well,' said Silver, 'you praise your stars he's dead.'

Suddenly, from the trees ahead, a thin, trembling voice sang:

'Fifteen men on the Dead Man's Chest –
    Yo-ho-ho and a bottle of rum!'

I have never seen men so dreadfully affected as these

pirates. The colour drained from their faces as they stared ahead in terror. Even Silver was shaking, but he was the first to pull himself together.

'I'm here to get that treasure!' he roared. 'I was never feared of Flint in his life, and by the Powers, I'll face him dead!'

With fresh heart, the men picked up their tools and set off again.

We soon saw ahead a huge tree that stood high above the others. The thought of what lay near that tree made the men's fears fade, and they moved faster. Silver hobbled on his crutch. I could tell from the evil in his eyes that, if he got his hands on the gold, he would cut all our throats.

The men now broke into a run, but not for long. They had come to the edge of a pit. At the bottom lay bits of wood and the broken handle of a pickaxe. It was clear for all to see that the treasure had gone!

The pirates jumped into the hole and began to dig with their hands. Silver knew that they would turn on him.

'We're in a tight spot, Jim,' he whispered. With the pirates against him, he needed me again.

The pirates scrambled out of the pit and stood facing Silver and me. The leader raised his arm to charge, but before a blow was struck, three musket shots rang out and two pirates fell. The other three men ran for their lives. We saw the Doctor coming out of the wood, followed quickly by Ben Gunn. They had saved us in the nick of time.

LAST WORDS

Silver and I were taken to Ben Gunn's cave, where the rest of our party was waiting. It was a happy moment for me to see all my friends again. My friends had been glad to move out of the log house to the safety of Gunn's cave.

We now learned the answer to the question that had puzzled Silver and me. Dr Livesey had found out that Ben Gunn, alone on the island for so long, had discovered the treasure and taken it to his cave. The map, then, had been useless.

And it was Ben Gunn's voice that had struck terror into the pirates' hearts with his ghostly song!

That night we all feasted and laughed and rested. Long John Silver, smiling quietly, became once more the polite and willing seaman I had first known.

The next day we began to pack the treasure into sacks, in preparation for loading it aboard the *Hispaniola*. There was a great mass of gold coins, from every part of the world, and transporting it all took several days. But at last we were ready to set sail for home.

We knew there were still three pirates somewhere on the island. We decided to leave them food and supplies, so that they could last until some ship found them.

And so we set sail. I cannot express the joy I felt as I watched Treasure Island disappear over the horizon.

We had not enough crew to sail the ship home and so we made for the nearest port in South America to find some extra men. We dropped anchor and went ashore, happy to be in a bright, busy place again.

When the Doctor, the Squire and I returned to the *Hispaniola*, Ben Gunn told us that Silver had taken a small amount of the treasure and gone. We were all glad to be rid of him. Our one wish now was to reach Bristol safely.

We had a good voyage home, and when we arrived, we shared out the treasure. Ben Gunn got a thousand pounds, which he spent or lost in less than three weeks. He was given a little job in the village, and he still sings in the church choir.

Of Long John Silver we never heard anything again. But sometimes, in a bad dream, I fancy I hear his parrot, Captain Flint, still screeching, 'Pieces of eight! Pieces of eight! Pieces of eight!'

OLIVER TWIST

by Charles Dickens
illustrated by John Holder

OLIVER'S EARLY LIFE

In the first half of the nineteenth century, there existed in most English towns a grim building known as the workhouse. This was where the parish authorities sent the aged, the homeless and the poor who could not work and had nowhere else to go.

It was in the workhouse that Oliver Twist was born. Oliver's mother, a beautiful young woman, had been found lying in the street the night before. No one knew who she was, and she died within minutes of giving birth. Oliver Twist was given his unusual name by Mr Bumble, the parish official in charge of the workhouse.

At the age of ten months, Oliver was sent out to a branch-workhouse, to be brought up by a Mrs Mann. She looked after twenty or thirty orphans, for a small weekly fee paid by the parish. Mrs Mann used most of this money for herself, and very little to feed and clothe the children. Consequently Oliver, like his comrades, grew into a small, pale, thin child.

When Oliver was nine, Mr Bumble took him back to the workhouse, to be taught a trade with other boys his age.

As miserable as Oliver had been at Mrs Mann's, he was even more unhappy

'Please, sir… I want some more'

at the workhouse. He missed his friends, and he was hungrier than he had ever been. All the boys were ever fed was gruel.

One evening, Oliver thought he would go mad with hunger. Desperately, with his bowl and spoon in hand, he approached the master of the workhouse.

'Please, sir,' he said, 'I want some more.'

The master was stupefied. No one ever dared to ask for more. *WHAT?'* he roared.

'Please, sir,' Oliver repeated quietly, 'I want some more.'

Enraged, the master struck Oliver on the head, and locked him up in a dank and dismal cell. He remained there for weeks and was rescued only when Mr Sowerberry, an undertaker, decided to take him as an apprentice.

At the Sowerberrys', Oliver was fed scraps and had to sleep among the coffins. Still, he didn't complain. But one day he got into a fight with Mr Sowerberry's surly assistant. Mr Sowerberry was so angry that he threatened to send Oliver back to the workhouse.

Oliver was terrified. He couldn't bear the thought of returning to the workhouse. So he decided to run away.

OLIVER COMES TO LONDON

Oliver Twist sat wearily on a doorstep and shivered. The sun was just rising over the town, and the chill of the night was still in the empty streets. Oliver was too exhausted to move. He had walked seventy long, hard miles since running away from Mr Sowerberry, and his feet were sore and bleeding. He ached all over, and he was weak with hunger. But even this was better than the workhouse.

An hour or two passed, and people began appearing in the streets. They saw the ragged and weary orphan sitting on the doorstep, but most looked away and hurried on.

Then, all of a sudden, Oliver felt that someone was staring at him. He glanced up and saw a snub-nosed, rough-looking boy standing close by, looking him up and down with sharp, ugly little eyes.

'Hello!' the boy greeted Oliver chirpily. 'What are you doing here?'

'I'm hungry and tired. I've been walking for seven days,' Oliver replied in a weak voice.

'Seven days!' the boy exclaimed.

Then, unexpectedly, he gave Oliver a kind look. 'You'll be wanting grub. Don't worry, I'll pay!'

The boy was as good as his word. When Oliver had wolfed down the first real meal he had had for days, the boy asked, 'Got any lodgings?'

'No,' said Oliver ruefully.

'I suppose you want somewhere to sleep tonight, then?' said the boy. 'I know a nice old gent who'll give you a bed for nothing – he knows me very well!'

Oliver accepted his offer gratefully.

'What's your name?' the boy wanted to know.

Oliver told him.

'Mine's Jack Dawkins – they call me the Artful Dodger!' the boy said proudly.

Oliver was none too sure that someone with a name like that was an honest person, but he was so grateful for the Dodger's help that he said nothing.

FAGIN'S GANG

What Oliver Twist did not know yet was that the Dodger belonged to a gang of pickpockets and robbers. Nor did he know that the Dodger's 'old gent', whose name was Fagin, was the ringleader of the gang.

Oliver and the Artful Dodger had to walk through a maze of dark, smelly, frightening streets to reach Fagin's house. Oliver was even more scared when he met Fagin, a very old, shrivelled-up creature with a villainous-looking face and a mass of matted red hair.

'Come in, come in, my boy!' Fagin said to Oliver when the Dodger introduced him. 'We're very glad to see you!'

Something about Fagin's voice made Oliver feel cold all over, but the old man seemed kind enough. He gave Oliver a meal, then showed him to an old mattress where he could sleep.

In the days that followed, the Dodger and other boys in Fagin's gang went out picking pockets. They brought back many handkerchiefs, pocketbooks and other objects, which Oliver was given to sort out. Oliver never suspected that these things were stolen until one day when he was allowed to go out with the Dodger and a boy called Charley Bates.

The boys seemed to wander aimlessly through the streets for a long time until, suddenly, the Dodger halted in a narrow passageway and drew his companions back against the wall.

'See that old fellow by the bookstall?' he whispered, pointing to a rich-looking gentleman on the other side of the passageway. 'He'll do for us.'

'Very nicely!' agreed Charley Bates.

Charley and the Dodger slipped across to where the old gentleman stood looking at a book. As Oliver watched in growing alarm, the Artful Dodger plunged his hand into the man's pocket, drew out a handkerchief and handed it to Charley. Then the two of them ran at full speed round the corner.

Oliver felt a tingle of terror at what he had seen. It was out and out stealing, and he was involved! He began to run away, but it was too late. The old gentleman, whose name was Mr Brownlow, had discovered that his expensive handkerchief was missing.

'Stop! Stop, thief!' he shouted. He set off after the fleeing Oliver, and was joined by a growing crowd of people. A big, rough-looking man soon overtook Oliver and gave him a hefty blow with his fist. Oliver fell sprawling in the mud.

NEW FRIENDS

Someone called a policeman; Oliver was bundled off to the nearest police station, and Mr Brownlow followed. Curiously, he seemed to regret the whole business, and said so when Oliver was taken before the magistrate, Mr Fang.

'This boy is not a thief, sir,' Mr Brownlow protested. 'Please deal kindly with him. I believe he is ill.'

Oliver did indeed look very unwell. All of a sudden, he fell to the floor in a faint.

Just then, an elderly man came rushing into the courtroom. 'Stop! Stop!' he cried.

'Who are you?' Mr Fang demanded.

'I keep the bookstall in the passageway,' the man explained. 'The robbery was committed by another boy, not this poor young fellow!' He pointed to Oliver, still unconscious on the floor.

Mr Fang frowned and grumbled, but he dismissed the charge against Oliver.

Oliver was thrown onto the pavement outside the courtroom, where he was soon found by Mr Brownlow.

'How pale he is!' said Mr Brownlow anxiously. 'And he's shivering – he must have a fever. Call a coach, somebody!'

The next thing Oliver knew was that he was in bed in a quiet, shady room. 'What place is this?' he murmured.

A plump, motherly-looking old lady appeared beside the bed. There was a sweet, loving expression on her face.

'Hush, dear!' she said softly. 'You must stay quiet now, or you will be ill again!'

The lady's name was Mrs Bedwin, and she was Mr Brownlow's housekeeper. For several more days, she looked after Oliver, until at last he was well enough to be visited by Mr Brownlow.

'And how do you feel now, dear boy?' the old gentleman wanted to know.

'Oh, much better, sir, and very grateful indeed for all your goodness to me!'

As Oliver spoke, Mr Brownlow kept staring at him. This poor, neglected waif reminded him of someone, but whom? Then the answer came to him.

Of course – the portrait! Mr Brownlow looked up at the picture hanging on the wall just above Oliver's head. It showed a pretty young lady. Mr Brownlow glanced at Oliver and gave a start.

'Mrs Bedwin!' he gasped. 'Don't you see? This boy – his eyes, his mouth, his expression – his whole face is the same as the face in the picture!'

'He Must Be Found'

Meanwhile, the Artful Dodger and Charley were in big trouble with Fagin for 'losing' Oliver in the street.

When they returned without him, Fagin flew into a rage and threatened to throttle both of them. Oliver now knew quite a lot about the gang and how they worked, so Fagin was worried in case the boy had 'peached' – that is, betrayed the gang to the police.

'He must be found!' Fagin stormed.

'But how?' Charley Bates asked. 'London's an enormous place. Where do we start?'

Fagin's fury suddenly faded away. A cunning gleam came into his eyes. 'Leave that to me, my boy,' he told Charley as he paced the room. 'I'll think of something!'

Fagin did not take long to come up with a plan. One of the thieves in the gang was a girl called Nancy. Fagin told her to go to the police station to see what she could find out about where Oliver was.

At first Nancy refused, for she was afraid of the police. She was more afraid, though, of Bill Sikes, another member of Fagin's gang and a cruel bully of a man.

'Say no, would you?' Bill glowered at Nancy, raising his hand. 'You'll get my fist in your face!' he threatened. It would not have been the first time Bill had beaten Nancy. 'All right, all right,' she said hastily. 'I'll go!'

If she had to run this errand, Nancy thought, she might as well make a good job of it. Nancy was a good actress, and when she got to the police station she burst into tears. Through her sobs, she told the policeman that she had lost her dear little brother. She was lying and meant Oliver, of course.

'Where is he? Oh, where is he?' Nancy wept. 'I must find him!'

Fagin flew into a rage

The policeman, a softhearted man, was totally deceived by Nancy's pretence. So he told her that the boy had been taken away by an old gentleman who lived near Pentonville in north London.

When Nancy returned with this news, Fagin immediately sent her out again, with the Artful Dodger and Charley Bates, to search for the house in Pentonville.

'Oliver has not betrayed us yet!' Fagin muttered. 'Nancy would've learned at the station if he had! But he must be found before he can talk, or we are all lost!'

But Oliver was going to fall into Fagin's hands much more easily than anyone thought. As he recovered his health, he tried to think of a way to repay all the loving care he had received in Mr Brownlow's house. His chance came one day when a messenger delivered some books for Mr Brownlow, but left before he could be given some other volumes which Mr Brownlow wanted to return to the shop.

'Please let me take them, sir!' Oliver begged. 'I won't be ten minutes! I'll run all the way!'

Oliver's eyes sparkled with eagerness as Mr Brownlow gave him the books and a five-pound note to cover the bill at the bookshop. He set off briskly, feeling very smart in the new clothes Mr Brownlow had bought for him. They were the first new clothes Oliver had ever worn, for in the workhouse he wore only ragged old clothes other people had discarded.

He had nearly reached the bookshop when a young woman suddenly stepped into his path. She flung her arms round his neck, and to his amazement she started crying, 'Oh, I've found him! My dear, lost little brother! I've found him!'

It was Nancy. She had just come out of a public house, where Fagin and Bill Sikes had been drinking and talking together. She was holding Oliver very tightly as he struggled hard, trying to escape.

'You're not my sister! I haven't got a sister!' Oliver kept yelling.

Just then, Mr Brownlow's books were snatched from him, and he felt a heavy blow on the back of his head. Bill Sikes had come out of the public house to see Oliver struggling with Nancy. Bill hit Oliver again, then grabbed his collar and began dragging the dazed boy through a maze of narrow, winding streets to the place that Oliver dreaded even more than the workhouse – Fagin's den.

'Delighted to see you looking so well, my boy!' Fagin said in a menacing voice that made Oliver shiver. He was trapped!

Oliver's heart sank when he thought of his new, kind friends at Mr Brownlow's house. What would they think when he did not return? Perhaps they would think he had run away with Mr Brownlow's

five pounds and the valuable books, to say nothing of his fine, new clothes.

'If they thought that, I could not bear it!' Oliver said to himself, distraught.

THREATENING WORDS

During the next few days, Fagin made certain that Oliver had no chance to escape.

All the while, Mr Brownlow was frantically searching for Oliver. He sent out servants to scour the streets for the boy, and asked everyone he met if they had seen him. He even put an advertisement in the newspaper, offering a reward for information about Oliver. But all his efforts achieved nothing. As far as Mr Brownlow knew, the boy had vanished.

In the meantime, Fagin was trying to train Oliver to be a thief telling him what a fortune he could make. Oliver did not believe him.

One day Fagin told Oliver, 'I'm sending you over to Bill Sikes, my boy! We've a nice little job for you!'

Nancy came to collect Oliver.

She seemed very upset, for she had become very fond of Oliver, and she knew that he was in great danger now. Fagin and Bill Sikes planned to use him to help them in a big robbery.

When they reached Bill's house, Bill took Oliver to one side. 'Do you know what this is?' he asked, showing Oliver a small pistol.

Oliver gulped and nodded. Bill picked up the pistol, loaded it and then placed the barrel against Oliver's head.

'We're going out, you and me,' Sikes

growled. 'And if you speak a word to anyone, I'll blow your head off!' It was not a threat Oliver could easily forget.

Bill Sikes took Oliver to a dank, dilapidated house well outside London. There, Sikes's two accomplices were waiting. After gathering up their pistols, crowbars and other equipment, they all set off into the pitch-black, foggy night.

Oliver now realised the frightful crime in which he was involved, and begged Bill Sikes to let him go. 'I'll never come near London again, I promise!' Oliver cried. 'Please, Mr Sikes, please!'

But Bill had a job for Oliver to do, and he meant to make sure he did it. When they reached the house where the robbery was going to take place, Bill forced open a tiny window with his crowbar. 'Get in there!' he told Oliver gruffly. 'Then open the front door and let us in. I'll point this pistol at you all the way, so don't try any tricks – or I'll shoot you dead!'

Despite this threat, Oliver decided to try and warn the people in the house. Once inside, he started running upstairs to the family's rooms. 'Come back, you wretch!' cried Bill Sikes.

All at once, two men appeared at the top of the stairs. One of them held a lantern, the other a pistol. Oliver heard him fire it, and felt a fierce, hot pain in his arm. Then there was a crash, another shot and the sound of a bell. Oliver felt himself being lifted up and dragged outside.

The burglary had gone wrong. The two men in the house had raised the alarm, and Bill Sikes and his gang could only run, taking Oliver with them.

Oliver was hardly aware of what was going on. He was dazed, and his arm hurt dreadfully. Blackness closed in on him, and he fainted.

KINDNESS – AND A DISAPPOINTMENT

When Oliver awoke, it was morning, and he was lying in a ditch, where Bill Sikes had left him. Bill and the other robbers were nowhere to be seen, for they had all managed to escape and had hurried back to London.

Oliver felt weak, and the shawl Bill had tied round his arm was soaked with blood. With a tremendous effort, he struggled to his feet and staggered along until he reached the road. A short way on, he came to a house. With a flicker of fear, he realised that it was the very house where the robbery had been attempted the previous night. Oliver wanted to run away, but his strength failed him.

Inside, the servants heard a noise. When they opened the front door, one of them, Mr Giles, recognised Oliver.

'Here's the thief! I shot him!' he shouted.

'Giles!' a soft voice whispered from the stairs. 'Hush, or you'll frighten my aunt!'

It was a young girl, very slender and sweet-faced, with kind, deep-blue eyes. She came quietly down the stairs and looked at Oliver, who had been carried inside and was lying on the hall floor.

'Oh, the poor little fellow!' the girl exclaimed. 'Carry him upstairs, Giles. Gently now, be careful!'

The young lady, whose name was Rose, sent for the doctor, who discovered that the bullet had broken Oliver's arm. It would be

'Gently now, be careful!'

a long time before the arm mended and Oliver was well again.

Rose, her aunt Mrs Maylie, the doctor, whose name was Losberne, and all the servants – even Giles – were very kind and gentle towards Oliver.

Though he was grateful for his good fortune, Oliver wanted more than anything to return to London and find Mr Brownlow.

Dr Losberne offered to take him to London in his carriage. When they reached the street where Mr Brownlow lived, Oliver spotted the house at once.

'That one! There! The white house!' he cried, pointing excitedly.

But Oliver's excitement soon faded, for the house was all shut up and there was a notice outside saying 'To Let'. Dr Losberne sent his coachman next door to make enquiries, and he returned with the sad news that Mr Brownlow had gone away six weeks previously, far across the Atlantic Ocean to the West Indies.

Oliver burst into tears. It was all too terrible! Mr Brownlow must have left thinking Oliver was a deceitful, little wretch. Now he would never learn the truth.

A CURIOUS TALE

Dr Losberne took Oliver back to his friends in the country, and for a long time the boy was very sad. But three months later, Dr Losberne took Oliver to London again, and Rose Maylie came with them. This time they were all delighted to discover that Mr Brownlow had returned and was very anxious for news of Oliver. The old gentleman greeted Oliver warmly, and Mrs Bedwin hugged and kissed him.

When all the greetings were over, and Oliver was occupied telling Mrs Bedwin of his adventures, Rose asked to see Mr Brownlow alone. Mr Brownlow took her to a quiet room, where she told him a curious tale.

A day or two before, a wretched young girl called Nancy had come to see Rose at her hotel in London. Nancy told Rose about a man called Monks, who had come to Fagin's house a few days earlier. Fagin and Monks knew each other already, for they had planned the burglary at the house where Rose and Mrs Maylie lived.

Fagin took Monks off to another room and Nancy, listening at the door, overheard them talking of Oliver. Monks said that Oliver was his brother, and he wanted Fagin to have him killed so that he could get his hands on the boy's fortune.

'I heard Monks mention your name, Miss,' Nancy had explained to Rose, 'and where you were staying in London. That's how I knew where to find you.' Then Nancy began to cry bitterly. 'Please, Miss, don't let Oliver come to any harm! I'd give my own life to save him. Honest I would!'

'But what can I do?' Rose had protested. 'How can I find this dreadful Mr Monks?'

'I can help you,' Nancy promised. 'Find a gentleman to help and protect you, and I'll tell you where to find Monks.'

'Where shall we meet you?' asked Rose.

'On London Bridge. I'll be there every Sunday night, between eleven and midnight,' Nancy said.

Mr Brownlow was intrigued by Rose's story. 'There's a mystery here, right enough,' he said. 'Nancy is taking a great risk for Oliver's sake. The evil thieves and criminals who are her companions will surely kill her if they discover what she has done. Still,' he went on, 'we cannot let this chance slip by. Oliver's fortune, and his life, are at stake. We must meet this girl and learn all we can from her!'

Nancy was not on London Bridge the first Sunday night, for Bill Sikes threatened to beat her if she left the house.

Fagin was there at the time, and he thought there was something very odd about Nancy's manner and behaviour. He decided to send one of his boys to follow Nancy on the next Sunday night, to see where she went and whom she met.

The spy faithfully carried out Fagin's instructions. He watched as Nancy met Rose and Mr Brownlow just after midnight. Creeping closer, he heard Nancy describe Mr Monks, the public house he often visited, and at what times.

'You can recognise him easily,' Nancy said. 'There is a mark on his throat, a big red...'

'A red mark!' Mr Brownlow interrupted. 'A mark like a burn or a scald?'

THE MYSTERY IS SOLVED

Monks was led to a back room.

'Go outside and lock the door!' Mr Brownlow told the menservants. 'Mr Monks and I will speak together alone.' The servants looked doubtful, for Monks seemed dangerous, but they still obeyed.

When they had gone, Mr Brownlow looked at Monks sadly.

I thought this was the man, Mr Brownlow reflected silently. *He's the son of my best friend. Nancy described him well.* Aloud he said, 'Your name is not Monks, it's Edward Leeford!'

Monks gave a start of surprise. 'How d'you know that?' he growled suspiciously.

Mr Brownlow sighed. 'Because I knew your father, Edwin Leeford, and his sister, who died many years ago – on the very day she and I were to be married!'

A flicker of pain quickly crossed Mr Brownlow's face as he remembered his young bride-to-be. 'I know that your father and mother were unhappy together, and that they parted when you were still a boy. And...' Mr Brownlow

'Why, yes!' Nancy replied. 'Do you know him?'

Mr Brownlow nodded grimly. 'Yes, yes, I think I do!' he muttered.

The very next day, Mr Brownlow went out with two menservants to look for Monks. Quite near the public house Nancy had mentioned, they spotted their prey.

Before Monks knew what was happening, the menservants grabbed him, bundled him into a hackney carriage and drove off to Mr Brownlow's house.

paused for a second. 'I know that you have a brother!'

Monks's eyes narrowed. 'I have no brother. I was an only child!'

'The only child of your father's marriage, yes!' said Mr Brownlow. 'But after your parents parted, your father fell in love with a beautiful young girl called Agnes Fleming. Poor Agnes died giving birth to their child – a boy who, by the grace of God, later fell into my hands! I knew what Agnes looked like, you see, for your father gave me her portrait, and the boy looked exactly like her!'

Monks was dumbfounded by these revelations. But Mr Brownlow had not yet finished. He told how Oliver had disappeared on the way to the bookshop, and how he had searched for him.

'I knew you could solve this mystery for me,' Mr Brownlow told Monks. 'I also knew of your criminal life and that you had escaped to the West Indies. So I followed you there!'

The voyage to the West Indies had been fruitless. By the time Mr Brownlow had arrived there, Monks had already returned to

England. When Mr Brownlow came home, he had scoured the streets seeking Monks for many weeks. But not until he heard Nancy speak of the man with the scar did the old gentleman have any clue to where Monks was.

'You were a wretched child, and you are still a scoundrel and a robber!' Mr Brownlow declared. 'You plan to have young Oliver murdered, don't you, so you can have all your father's money!'

'You can't prove anything against me!' Monks blustered, turning very pale.

'Oh, but I can!' Mr Brownlow retorted. 'I know about Fagin and the plot you hatched together!'

'F-Fagin?' said Monks. 'Who is he?'

'Shall we call the police, then, and let you deny it to them?'

Monks looked terrified. 'No, no, don't!' he pleaded. 'They'll hang me!'

'Ah, then you will do as I demand!' cried Mr Brownlow. 'You must sign a document giving Oliver his rightful share of your father's money!'

Monks thought miserably of the police cell, the courtroom and the hangman's rope that

72

would surely be his lot if he refused. 'Very well,' he muttered. 'Oliver shall have his inheritance – I promise!'

A BRIGHT FUTURE

Sadly, poor Nancy paid a high price for the risks she had taken on Oliver's behalf. When Fagin's spy told him about Nancy's meeting with Rose and Mr Brownlow, Fagin had been enraged. He told Bill Sikes the whole story. Bill took his pistol and coldheartedly shot Nancy dead.

Even as Mr Brownlow and Monks were talking, the police were out hunting for the murderer. That very night, they cornered Bill Sikes in his hiding place. In a panic, Bill clambered out onto the roof, taking a rope to help him make his escape. But he slipped, and as he fell, the rope tangled round his neck, choking him to death.

That same day, acting on information given to them by Mr Brownlow, the police arrested Fagin. At his trial, Fagin was condemned to die on the gallows.

As for Oliver Twist, Mr Brownlow adopted him as his own son and took him

to live in the country. Oliver loved the fresh, green countryside, with its beautiful fields and flowers and trees.

Once, Oliver had been a poor, misused orphan whose only home was the workhouse. Now, his future was bright and life offered him much happiness. He had the inheritance his father had intended for him. Above all, now that Fagin was dead and his gang broken up, Oliver need never be afraid of them again.

ROBIN HOOD

retold by John Grant
illustrated by Victor G Ambrus

ROBIN THE OUTLAW

Robin of Locksley was a Saxon gentleman. He lived near Nottingham, on the edge of Sherwood Forest.

The King of England, Richard the Lionheart, was a Norman, as were most English nobles of the time. The ordinary people were Saxons, and many were treated harshly by their cruel and greedy Norman lords. King Richard, who should have punished the wrongdoers, was off fighting in the Holy Land. In his place he had left his brother, Prince John... the cruellest and greediest Norman of all.

Early one summer's day, Robin of Locksley left his home, Locksley Hall. Not all Normans were wicked, and one of Robin's friends was a young Norman lady, Marian Fitzwalter. She was returning from a visit, and her way led through Sherwood Forest.

The forest was a dangerous place, where travellers risked attack and robbery by outlaws. Robin had agreed to meet Marian and her servants, and escort them on the last few miles to her father's house. Shouldering his longbow and arrows, he made his way towards the shady forest.

Robin scanned the ground for signs that might warn of danger. At first there

Robin of Locksley was a Saxon gentleman

where it ran through a hollow. Now he could hear faint sounds of movement. Inching forwards, he looked down into the hollow. Almost hidden among the bushes was a group of armed men. Beyond the road, he could just make out the shape of a horse and rider. It was an ambush – and Marian Fitzwalter was riding right into it!

I must stop her! thought Robin. Circling round, he reached the edge of the road just below the hollow. A moment later, Marian and her servants came into sight.

Robin shouted a warning, but in the same instant an armed horseman crashed through the bushes, blocking Marian's way. Marian's horse reared up in fright as men-at-arms sprang out on all sides to form a semicircle across the road.

His bow at the ready, Robin leapt between Marian and the horseman. 'Clear the way, knight,' he shouted, 'and let the lady pass freely!'

'Locksley! Saxon dog! Stand aside!' snarled the knight, sword in hand. The next moment he fell from the saddle, an arrow through his heart.

The men-at-arms closed in. In the blink of an eye, Robin fired three more arrows, and three of the attackers were slain.

were only deer tracks. But when he came to a broad path, the ground was churned up by footprints and hoof marks. A sizable party had passed this way not long before, and it looked as if they planned to join the main forest road – the road on which Marian Fitzwalter was travelling.

Robin continued down the path. The travellers could not be far ahead, yet he heard no sound. Whatever their purpose, they were going very carefully about their business. He began to feel uneasy.

Soon Robin was close to the road,

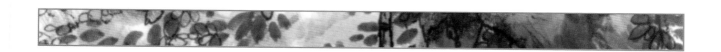

Robin fitted another arrow to his bow, but the rest of the men had fled. They dared not face Robin of Locksley, the most accurate bowman in the Sheriffdom of Nottingham – if not all England.

Marian looked down at the dead knight. 'Roger de Mortmain,' she said. 'One of my family's most bitter enemies!'

'We must hurry now,' said Robin. 'There may be others of de Mortmain's people looking out for you. The sooner I bring you to your father, the better.'

It was midday before they came in sight of Malaset Manor, the home of the Fitzwalters. After Marian and her father greeted each other, Robin described what had happened.

'Robin of Locksley,' said Sir Richard Fitzwalter, 'you have done my family a great service. Roger de Mortmain was an evil man. No reward I could offer would be high enough. But you have put yourself in great danger – killing a Knight of the Realm is a grave offence. The Sheriff of Nottingham is bound to issue a warrant for your arrest. You must flee at once. Go into hiding.'

'No,' replied Robin. 'The Sheriff, or his crony Guy of Gisborne, is more likely to take revenge on me by attacking my people. I must return to Locksley without delay!' And he set off with all speed and urgency towards Locksley Hall.

He was nearing the edge of the woodland and the open fields when he heard a rustle in the undergrowth. A voice called softly, 'Master! Master Locksley! Over here!'

Robin knew the voice. It was Will Scarlett, a poacher by trade, and no friend to the royal foresters. He was dusty and dishevelled, with blood on his face from a cut cheek.

'You must go no further,' Scarlett said. 'Gisborne's men are lying in wait for you. They say you have committed a terrible crime, and they have laid waste to Locksley.'

'What of my people?' asked Robin anxiously.

'They had some warning,' said Will. 'The families escaped to nearby villages. But four of the men were taken prisoner.'

'Gisborne trusts that I will come to their rescue,' said Robin. 'I won't disappoint him.'

They hurried to the Manor of

Locksley – or what was left of Robin's former home. Smoke still rose from the ruins. Stables, cottages and barns lay wrecked. The mill smouldered darkly in the distance.

'Mutch the miller's son was taken,' said Will. 'Gilbert the ditcher and Nic the carter, too.'

'How many of Gisborne's men are still there?' asked Robin. 'How are they armed?'

'Six stayed behind with the prisoners, armed with swords only,' said Will.

Robin thought for a moment. 'Here's what you must do, Will,' he said, and whispered something to him. Will nodded, picked up his bow and slipped away through the trees.

Robin strode across the open ground to the rubble-strewn courtyard of the ruined Hall.

'That's far enough, Saxon!'

A sergeant and two men-at-arms stepped out from behind the burning gable. Robin glimpsed three more, partly hidden by the wall. *All six*, he thought. *Good. The prisoners may be bound, but they are unguarded. Probably close by…*

'Ah, sergeant!' Robin called.

'Had I known you were visiting, I would have stayed to welcome you to my humble home.'

'Home?' laughed the sergeant. 'You call a murdering Saxon rat's bolt-hole a home?'

'Serving in Gisborne Castle,' replied Robin, 'you must know all about rat holes!'

'Enough talk, Robin of Locksley!' shouted the sergeant. 'You are under arrest, for the heinous crime of murder.'

'And who will arrest *you*?' retorted Robin. 'There has long been a law about burning people's houses…'

'Seize him!' cried the sergeant.

The men-at-arms ran forwards. Robin met them, sword in hand. One went down to a thrust through his sword arm. A second reeled back, dazed from the flat of Robin's blade across his neck.

The other men-at-arms rushed to join the fight. Ash and smoke swirled through the air as Robin fought off the attack. He was greatly outnumbered. Where was Will Scarlett?

Suddenly one of the soldiers screamed and fell, transfixed by an arrow. Men were shouting and

charging across the courtyard: Will with his bow, and four other men throwing stones and pieces of wood.

'I have a good Saxon arrow for the man who is last to drop his sword!' shouted Will.

But before anyone could move, Mutch cried, 'Back!' and dragged Robin by the sleeve. The Saxons scrambled clear, as the fire-weakened gable of Locksley Hall crashed to the ground. The sergeant and his men-at-arms vanished under a heap of broken stone in a cloud of smoke and ash.

From the edge of the forest, Robin looked back. 'I have nothing now,' he said to the men around him, 'but my sword and my longbow. Locksley is no more. I am Robin the outlaw now.'

'We are all outlaws,' said Will Scarlett, 'including Hal, here. He brought us warning.'

The man nodded. 'Hal the fletcher,' he said. 'I was delivering arrows to the Gisborne garrison when I heard the orders being given. I came as quickly as I could.' Hal grinned. 'I stole one of Gisborne's horses to speed my way.'

Mutch laughed. 'Here am I, a miller without a mill, *and* an outlaw. My companions? A murderer, a poacher and a horse thief. A merry company indeed!'

Led by Will Scarlett, the small band entered Sherwood Forest. As a poacher, Will knew every secret path and hidden glade. The sun was setting when he called a halt. They were in a wide clearing. A stream flowed nearby. A high rock stood like a watchtower to one side.

'I suggest we camp here tonight,' said Will.

Nic lit a fire. Will went off with his bow and returned shortly with the carcass of

Robin called the men together

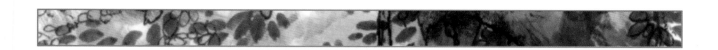

a young stag. 'Tonight we dine on royal venison,' he cried, 'as served at the table of our true king... Richard the Lionheart.'

'And of his evil brother, John,' said Gilbert.

'But not in such fine company,' laughed Mutch.

They all fetched water from the stream in their hats – all, that is, except Robin.

'I have no hat,' he said, 'only the hood of my jerkin.'

Mutch laughed again. 'Then I would be honoured to share mine with you, Robin o' the Hood!'

'Yes!' cried Will Scarlett. 'Robin of Locksley is dead. Long live our leader – Robin o' the Hood!'

LITTLE JOHN

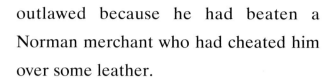

Mutch's nickname for Robin of Locksley stuck – only shortened to 'Robin Hood'. The band of outlaws grew quickly. Some were men of Locksley, like Will Stutely. Others were tradesmen, like Arthur Bland, a tanner from Nottingham. He was

outlawed because he had beaten a Norman merchant who had cheated him over some leather.

One day, Robin called the men together. 'There are almost forty of us now,' he said. 'We are all wanted men. So we must be ready to fight for our freedom. We must also fight to defend the poor, the weak and the helpless.'

'But how can we fight?' asked Nic. 'None of us are warriors, and we have no weapons.'

'Then you must learn,' said Robin. 'First you will learn how to fight with quarterstaves. We have a champion in our midst – right, Mutch?'

'I did win a prize at Nottingham Fair,' Mutch confessed, blushing.

'Right,' said Robin. 'I appoint Mutch as quarterstaff instructor. Each man will cut an ash staff for himself. Then somehow we must find swords, bows and arrows for us all. We will be a small army, but to keep order we must have rules,' he went on. 'First, our enemies are greed and cruelty.'

'And Normans,' said Will.

'Not all Normans,' Robin pointed out. 'We can count on

some Normans as friends – the Fitzwalters of Malaset, for instance. There are also many cruel and greedy Saxons. All who travel through Sherwood Forest should be invited to contribute money or goods for the weak and helpless. And if they don't like the invitation, then they will be, let's say, persuaded,' said Robin, grinning.

'I see!' cried Mutch. 'Our first rule: rob the rich to feed the poor! And, as we are poor, we shall also feed ourselves. Very simple, really.'

Robin continued. 'Peasants, farmers, squires, knights, pilgrims and beggars may pass freely, except those whom we know to be villains or troublemakers.'

The outlaws took it in turns to keep watch from a high rock. One morning there was a shout from the lookout.

'Something is moving along the Nottingham road!' he called. 'The birds and animals are very disturbed. It may be a company of considerable number!'

'Dick!' Robin called to one of the young outlaws. 'Keep out of sight and find out who is taking the high road to Nottingham.'

Within an hour, Dick was back. 'A covered ox cart,' he reported, 'with an armed guard of eight soldiers – four riding in front, and four behind.'

The slow-moving cart and its escort stopped in a clearing near a charcoal-burner's hut.

'Hey! Charcoal-burner!' bellowed the captain of the escort. 'Which is the road to Nottingham, peasant?'

There was no reply. The captain dismounted, strode over to the hut, and banged hard on the door. At the same moment, an arrow thudded into the wood, a hair's breadth from his fist.

The captain whirled round. A second arrow hit the door on his other side, close to his shoulder. The captain drew his sword and started to shout an order. But a third arrow grazed the top of his helmet, then struck the door above his head.

'I shall give the orders!' called a voice from among the trees. 'You are surrounded. And we have more arrows than you have soldiers!'

Half-hidden behind every tree and bush, the soldiers could make out the figure of a man.

The mysterious voice gave the orders, and the soldiers dismounted and dropped their swords. Frightened, they crowded into the small, dark hut. Then the door was closed and wedged shut from outside.

Once the door was secure, Robin and the outlaws came out into the open and uncovered the cart. It was loaded with long, wooden crates.

Hal opened a crate. 'Arrows!' he exclaimed. 'And bows!' There were also swords and sword belts – all destined for Nottingham Castle.

The outlaws emptied the cart. Two to a crate, they started back to the camp.

Robin and Will Scarlett gathered up the weapons dropped by the escort. 'I believe in telling the truth,' said Robin, laughing. 'We did have more arrows – but only two bows!'

He crossed to the charcoal-burner's hut. 'Robin Hood thanks the Sheriff for his generosity,' he called to his Norman prisoners. 'Long before you manage to break free, we shall be far away. We leave you your cart and horses. It is a long walk from here to Nottingham, and in any case animals and prisoners are too much trouble for us to feed and guard. 'Goodbye, and safe journey to you all!'

The Sheriff of Nottingham raged when the news reached him. Prince John was even more furious. 'Robin Hood! That's all I hear!' he shouted. 'My own stable boys and scullions speak of no one else!'

By training and practising every day, the outlaws became adept with their new weapons. Soon there were few to equal them at quarterstaff, swordplay and archery.

Grasping, greedy landlords and harsh Norman overseers found themselves waylaid on forest roads and persuaded to hand over

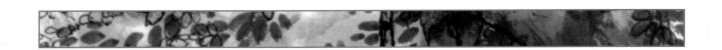

their money. Gifts of money, food and clothing were often left mysteriously at the doors of cottages in peasant villages.

Some men of the Church, who should have known better, grew fat on the toil of the peasants who worked the Church lands, and increased their rents. One day, Robin and his men had ambushed the Abbey's rent collectors to recover some peasants' money. Now they were returning to camp.

The track they were following came out into a broad meadow through which flowed a wide, deep stream. A fallen tree made a bridge.

As usual when crossing open ground, the outlaws were very cautious. Robin went first, hurrying towards the tree-bridge. He was just turning to signal the others to follow him, when they heard a loud shout from the far bank.

A tall, burly man stood with one foot on the fallen tree. 'One moment, friend!' he shouted. 'I want to cross!'

'By all means!' Robin called back. 'As soon as I've come over, the way is free for you to cross.'

'No, no!' shouted the tall man. 'I have right of way, as I have already set foot on the bridge.

Step aside like a good fellow.' And he laughed and twirled a long staff in front of him.

Robin unslung his bow. 'I do not yield to threats!' he said angrily.

'Then let us dispute it man to man!' cried the other. 'But I am unarmed except for my staff. Bow against quarterstaff is hardly fair.' He laughed again.

Robin laid his bow and quiver on the ground. 'Lend me your quarterstaff, Nic,' he called. The outlaws came out into the open, and Nic tossed Robin his ash staff.

The two men advanced to the middle of the log. 'Now, archer, let's see you really fight!' laughed Robin's opponent. Robin used all his skill, but he could not land a single blow. Neither could the other, though he was a head taller and had a longer reach than Robin.

The forest echoed to the crack of staves as each man swung and parried. Then Robin slipped and lost his balance. With a resounding splash, he tumbled into the deep water.

The big man peered into the stream. Robin was nowhere to be seen. 'I hope I haven't drowned your friend,' the man said to the

The forest echoed to the crack of staves

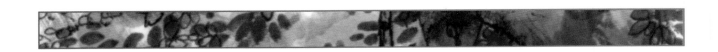

outlaws. 'I rather liked him…' His voice broke off with a yell as Robin, who had surfaced from the water, grabbed his ankle. Another splash, and the two of them stood up and waded, laughing, to the bank.

Robin pointed to the bridge. 'The road is clear,' he said. 'You may continue on your way now.'

'In a moment,' said the man, 'when I get my breath and empty my boots of water.'

The outlaws crossed to join them. Nic asked the man, 'Where are you bound?'

'To find my cousin,' said the big man. 'I heard he was in these parts. Wanted by the law. Trouble with a cheating Norman leather merchant. Arthur Bland, he's called. Perhaps you've heard of him.'

'Heard of him? He's one of our company!' laughed Robin.

'Then you must be Robin Hood!' exclaimed the big man. 'I'm John Little, until recently a cattleman from near Mansfield. I'm in much the same sort of trouble as cousin Arthur – a Norman steward got in the way of my fist! You're not recruiting, by any chance, are you, Master Hood?'

'Well,' grinned Robin, 'you may join us on one condition.

We are a merry company and fond of a joke. You will forget that you were ever John Little and from this day you will be known as "Little John". Agreed?'

'Agreed,' said the new outlaw. 'Little John I shall be – in name, if not in size or deed!'

Little John became a popular member of the band. None could be down at heart in his company, and he was a strong and fearless fighter. In time, he would become Robin Hood's right-hand man.

THE SILVER ARROW

One of Robin Hood's friends was a monk, Brother Anselm. Robin once asked him, 'Why not join us here in the forest? Like our good King Richard, we are God-fearing Christians, and we need a chaplain.'

Brother Anselm replied, 'My work is with the sick in the Abbey infirmary. But perhaps you should seek out Brother Tuck of Copmanhurst. He has upset the Abbot of St Mary's by refusing to accept a fee for marrying people. And he often brings a haunch of venison to the wedding feast, so he is an enemy of the royal foresters, too. Instead of "Brother", he calls himself by the French title "Friar" – Friar Tuck.'

A few days later, Robin, with Little John and half a dozen others, set off to find Friar Tuck. Near Copmanhurst Forest they came to a stream. There, holding a fishing line, was a burly man with a shaved head and a monk's habit.

Robin approached him. 'Holy man,' he said, 'I wish to cross the stream. Will you, like good Saint Christopher, carry me?'

'As you wish,' said the monk, leaning over so Robin could climb on his back. He waded into the stream and quickly crossed it. 'Now,' said Robin, 'I would be obliged if you would take me back again.'

Without a word, the monk retraced his steps. But halfway across, he made a sudden move to throw Robin off his back.

Robin gripped hard with his arms and legs. 'Not quite yet, my friend,' he said. 'I prefer to reach the bank dry-shod.'

'As you please,' the monk laughed. As they reached the water's edge, he suddenly dropped onto one knee. Robin flew through the air and hit the ground

with a thump, but he was on his feet in time to grab the monk in a wrestler's hold.

With one skilful throw, the monk put Robin flat on the ground. Robin realised that he had met his match as a wrestler.

'Submit?' asked the monk, sitting on Robin to hold him down.

'I submit!' replied Robin. 'For a man of the Church you are a fearsome wrestler!'

'We men of God are required to wrestle with Satan. Wrestling with men is good practice,' chuckled the monk.

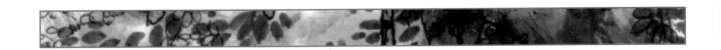

As they all made their way to the monk's shack, Robin said, 'So you are Friar Tuck!'

'The same,' said Tuck. 'And you, I am certain, are Robin Hood. I'm not sure that an outlaw is fit company for a man of peace.' But he grinned cheekily as he spoke, and fetched mugs and a firkin of ale.

Robin looked round. For a man of peace, Tuck was well equipped. A sword hung on a wall.

'Will you join us?' Robin asked the Friar.

'I'll think about it,' said Tuck. 'It can be lonely here – except when Gisborne's men come bothering me!'

When the outlaws rose to go, Tuck rose, too. 'I'll accompany you part of the way,' he said.

They had gone barely a mile when they heard men shouting, horses neighing and the clash of weapons. 'Listen!' said Little John. 'Someone's in trouble!'

They hurried towards the noise, and saw a milling crowd of men and horses engaged in battle. Some of the men wore livery and were armed.

'Gisborne's cutthroats!' cried Tuck. 'And my sword left hanging on the wall!' He picked up a stout tree branch and charged. The outlaws could hardly keep up with him.

One of the attackers was trying to pull a white-haired man from his horse. Tuck briskly whirled the branch round and sent the attacker spinning.

Taken by surprise, Gisborne's men were quickly overcome. Some fled, others were brought down by well-aimed arrows.

'I'm in your debt,' said the white-haired man. 'I'm Simon of Lincoln. Those villains would have stolen the goods I was taking to Nottingham market.'

One of Simon's people was badly hurt. 'You must rest before continuing,' Robin said. 'Be our guest tonight, and tomorrow we will see you safely to Nottingham.'

Next morning, Simon told Robin and his men, 'I owe you a great deal, including my life. I must reward you. Most of you could use some new garments. Perhaps this will help.' He took from one of his horses a bolt of fine, dark green woollen cloth. 'This is woven in my own town. We call it Lincoln green,' he explained.

Escorted by Will Scarlett, Simon and his people went on their way.

When Will returned, he had some news. 'Prince John is holding an archery contest,' he said, 'to find the champion bowman of all England. The prize is a silver arrow.'

Little John frowned. 'This is no ordinary contest,' he said. 'Why hold it in a small town like Nottingham? I think Prince John has only one purpose... to lure Robin into a trap.'

'You may be right,' said Robin, 'but I must take part. A Saxon champion would be a great thing for the ordinary

people – and, better still, a blow to John and his Norman cronies.'

On the day of the contest, the outlaws made their way to Nottingham. Robin wore old, shabby clothes. His face, grimy with wood ash, was hidden by a long, hooded cloak. His hair was uncombed. He looked like a beggar.

Stands had been erected, and targets were set up. Busy stalls sold food and drink. Flags flew over the colourful pavilions of the nobility. Over the largest pavilion flew the standard of the sly Prince John. There the Prince and the Sheriff of Nottingham sat, muttering to one another as they watched the competitors gather for the archery contest.

Amidst all this splendour, people crowded from far and near, eager to see who would be declared champion. Soldiers of the garrison kept a close watch on the crowd. But the outlaws came in ones and twos, their weapons hidden under their cloaks, so they attracted no attention.

At last the contest began. There were more than eighty contestants. Steadily they were eliminated until only four were left, including Robin.

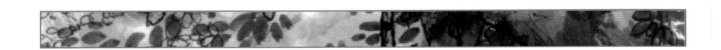

As Little John watched anxiously, there was a tug at his sleeve. 'Master Simon!' he exclaimed.

'You must all get away, now!' said the merchant. 'A troop of Gisborne's mounted men are hidden behind the royal pavilion. They will attack as soon as you leave.'

Little John looked round for the others. But he could not see them in the crowd – and the final part of the contest was about to begin.

The targets for this part were willow wands, set upright in the ground. An arrow that did not strike true would glance off the slippery wood and not count as a hit.

In the royal stand, Prince John and the Sheriff of Nottingham kept watching the competitors for signs that one might be Robin Hood.

All at once, the Prince sat up. 'That is our man,' he said, pointing.

'Do you mean the beggar, Your Highness?' asked the Sheriff.

'No beggar stands so proud in front of his betters,' said the Prince. 'If that is not Robin Hood, then I am not John Lackland!'

The first archer prepared to shoot. Thinking quickly, Little John whispered to one of his Saxon neighbours, 'They say the tall one is Robin Hood!'

The Saxon whispered excitedly to others around him, and soon the whispers ran all through the crowd: 'Robin Hood? Is it? Yes, surely! It is! It's Robin Hood!'

There was a hush as the first archer loosed an arrow. He missed. So did the second man. There was a gasp as the third archer's arrow grazed the willow wand, but then it too hit the ground. Now it was the turn of the hooded beggar.

A great roar of applause went up from the crowd as the beggar's arrow split the willow cleanly. Prince John stood up.

'Step forward, archer!' he cried. 'Champion bowman of all England… by a lucky shot!'

'Lucky!' cried Robin. In one smooth movement he turned and shot another arrow. It hit the first squarely and split it neatly in two.

The Prince sneered. 'I knew you would be unable to resist… Robin Hood!'

'Guards!' shouted the Sheriff. 'Arrest him!'

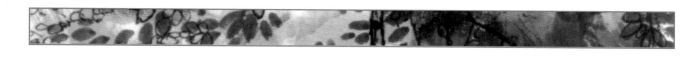

But his voice was lost in the crowd's roar. The guards were swept aside by a cheering mob of Saxons. The outlaws pushed their way to Robin; Little John had managed to tell them of Gisborne's trap. As the crowd spilled out from the archery ground, the outlaws were swept along in the confusion.

Tents collapsed, booths overturned and Gisborne saw his carefully planned ambush in ruins. His men-at-arms tried to force their way through the mob, but their horses, startled by the uproar, plunged and reared. When the Saxons began hurling pieces of the wrecked booths, the horsemen backed off.

As the outlaws raced for the forest, they could hear the hoofbeats of six horses, led by Guy of Gisborne, rapidly closing in on them.

Robin, Little John, Mutch and Nic formed a rear guard while the others sprinted for cover. Suddenly Little John went down, wounded by an arrow in the leg. Mutch ran to his aid, just managing to drag him towards the trees. They were pursued by a single horseman.

Robin raised his bow and shot; the horseman crashed down.

It was Guy of Gisborne!

'You didn't kill him!' cried Gilbert in disbelief.

'When the time comes, Guy of Gisborne and Robin of Locksley will meet in combat face to face,' said Robin. 'But now, I still have some unfinished business with Prince John.'

'Prince John?' asked Will Scarlett.

'Yes,' grinned Robin. 'He forgot to present me with my silver arrow!'